The Charity
Paperback Copyright © 2022 Lorhainne Ekelund
Editor: Talia Leduc

ISBN-13: 9781998775019

Give feedback on the book at:
lorhainneeckhart@hotmail.com

Twitter: @LEckhart
Facebook: AuthorLorhainneEckhart

Printed in the U.S.A

The Charity

BILLY JO MCCABE MYSTERY
BOOK NINE

LORHAINNE ECKHART

Nothing As It Seems
Hiding in Plain Sight
The Cold Case
The Trap
Above the Law
The Stranger at the Door
The Children
The Last Stand
The Charity
The Sacrifice

The social worker and the cop, an unlikely couple drawn together on a small, secluded Pacific Northwest island where nothing is as it seems. Protecting the innocent comes at a cost, and what seems to be a sleepy, quiet town is anything but.

The Social Worker

Billy Jo McCabe wants only to help children overcome their troubled lives, as she herself struggles to forget the childhood nightmare she survived. She took sociology and prelaw at the insistence of her adoptive father, Chase McCabe, and learned how to use power tools from her adoptive mother, Rose. She loves reading in the backs of bookstores before tucking the book back on the shelf and slipping out without paying. She has a fondness for peanut butter and dill pickle sandwiches, has a three-legged cat named Harley, hates running (because that was all she did as a kid), and secretly binges on brownies and red wine on the sofa in front of her TV every Friday night.

She's never been married and has dated only twice. She visits Chase and Rose when summoned and shows up dutifully for every holiday with her family, but she has no siblings to speak of, and she feels a growing resentment for the mother who abandoned her in foster care. Despite proudly maintaining the same prickly attitude that nearly landed her behind bars as a kid, she has yet to speak up to Chase, who interferes in her life too frequently, ready to fix every problem, whether she wants him to or not.

One thing no one knows about Billy Jo is that she moved to Roche Harbor because it's the only clue she has about the last known whereabouts of the woman who abandoned her.

The Cop

Mark Friessen, son of Jed and Diana Friessen, has landed accidently in the role of small-town detective, a position in which he's going nowhere. Nearly married once, and broken-hearted three times, he's sworn he'll stay single forever, and he keeps his tattoo of a former girlfriend as a reminder that only fools fall in love. He's tall, attractive, and stubborn, and he refuses to live in the shadow of his two older brothers, Chris and Danny.

As Roche Harbor's youngest detective, he sleeps with a gun under his pillow. He has a stray dog that won't leave, and he swears that the only two food groups that exist are meat and potatoes. His favorite drink is black coffee in the morning, sugared coffee in the afternoon, and a shot of whiskey in his coffee at night to keep him warm.

****Each book in this series is a complete book, with no cliff-hangers, and can be read as a standalone. However, these books may contain references to situations from earlier books in the series. As with any long book series that focuses on specific characters, their changing relationships, and how their lives continue to unfold, you may find it more enjoyable to read the series in order of publishing, as there will be developments and changes in the relationship dynamics of the core characters.*

Some secrets aren't meant to be told.

Police Chief Mark Friessen and his wife, social worker Billy Jo McCabe, keep a watchful eye on their small island town in the Pacific Northwest. As the couple comes to grips with the fact that a hub of crime run by the political elite has turned the quiet, sleepy Roche Harbor into a playground for the rich and powerful, a young executive of a major international charity moves to town. When Mark and Billy Jo dig deep into the secrets and lies that seem to follow the man, they uncover a twisted truth, one they may wish they had never found.

Newlyweds Mark Friessen and Billy Jo McCabe are back home in the town of Roche Harbor, settling into their life as a married couple while coming to grips with the evil that has woven its web in their small community. Police Chief Mark keeps a watchful eye on all the residents, learning who comes and goes on his island, so when a stranger buys a large property on the west side, Mark shows up on his doorstep to find out why he has moved in.

Walter Crandall tells him the island is home to his five-year-old daughter and his ex-wife, who owns a local bar, and all he wants is to keep a low profile and be left alone to make amends for his mistakes. But there's something about the man that Mark doesn't trust, and when he and Billy Jo begin digging into Walter's past and the charity he was part of, they uncover a deception so twisted they're convinced it can't possibly be true.

CHAPTER

One

Sleeping in was something Billy Jo didn't do, but for the past four days, Mark had opened his eyes to find his wife sound asleep. As he stood in the kitchen, the stove blinking a digital blue 8:10 a.m., he realized he needed to wake her soon.

The coffeemaker beeped, and Mark poured himself a cup of the steaming brew before turning back to the island, on which a file lay open, revealing notes on another thirty of the island's residents. Hesitating only a second, he wondered when he'd become that cop who went digging into civilians' lives, looking for any secrets they might have.

Oh, yeah. When a bunch of criminal elites took up using his island as their personal playground.

He had to roll his shoulders, feeling that punch in the gut again, silently hating the world of people who, at times, were untouchable.

"You didn't wake me."

He turned to see Billy Jo in a blue robe, yawning as she walked sock-footed past him and pulled a glass from the cupboard to fill with water.

"Figured you needed sleep," he said. "Was going to give you another ten minutes before waking you. You feeling okay?"

She brushed her shoulder-length brown bed hair away from her face and shook her head before drinking down the water. "Fine. Just tossed and turned because of your snoring. What are you doing?"

She settled her glass in the sink, then reached for his coffee and took a swallow of it. As she looked down at the open file, her brow furrowed. He realized she wasn't giving the coffee back, and he couldn't believe she had tossed out that comment about his snoring, considering she had fallen asleep before him.

He leaned down and pressed a kiss to the top of her head, then filled a second mug, a matching green one, from the many wedding gifts that seemed to still be arriving daily from people on the island he'd met only a time or two.

"Looking into the folks who live here," he said, "why they live here, what they do, especially the ones who look too clean. Who lives here full time, part time, and what hidden secrets do they have? You know, the usual investigative thing I do, looking for red flags and skeletons."

Mark filled the mug with coffee and settled the carafe back on the burner. Billy Jo angled her head, glancing over to him in that way of hers. She was complex, with many moods, and he figured something else was coming.

"You were serious, then?" she said, flattening her hand over the file, the notes he'd been reading on Shirley and Tom Campbell, and pulling it closer to her. "You're really going to investigate every person who lives here and dissect their lives even though they've done nothing wrong? Isn't there some law against that, let alone the fact that you're overstepping a bit?"

She didn't smile and didn't pull that fiery gaze from him. She was the complete package, a woman who was his best friend, his lover, his wife, and she knew how to push every one of his buttons. Damn, he loved everything about her.

He reached for the file in front of her and pulled it away. "Knowing who's on this island and what they're about is something I should have done long ago. You forget what happened here? I don't want that kind of evil ever sneaking in. So yeah, I plan to dissect the lives of everyone who lives here to make sure the members of this community are decent, honest, not looking to set up some criminal enterprise, thinking they can do anything. And that includes our politicians. Consider it my new pastime. I plan to find out everything about them, what they do, who they see, to really dig into their lives. If they are honest people, then they become the people I'm protecting. But how many more criminals are still here, so deep underground that I haven't found them yet? And *yet* is the key word."

She looked up at him, and a smile touched her lips as she leaned against the island, so close to him. "You know all the right things to say sometimes," she said. "Go dig and dissect the lives of anyone and everyone. Oh, and make sure, will you, that you take a second and third look at everyone collecting a check from the DCFS, and especially who rubber-stamped their approvals?"

"They're first on the list—kids and animals." He leaned down and kissed her forehead.

"You're the best," she said. "Damn, I'm going to be late." She lifted the mug and took a swallow. "Oh, and I forgot to tell you we're going to drop in and see Gail tonight. I'll swing by the station after I'm done and we'll head over. I told her we'll bring dinner…"

She had trailed off as she walked back to the bedroom.

Then she turned in the doorway, looking back, when he hadn't said anything. The tightness that came every time he thought of Tolly Shephard returned deep in his chest. He knew he'd made a face.

"You have to figure out a way to get past that, Mark," she said. "Gail is our friend."

"Her husband was part of a child trafficking ring."

She let out a heavy sigh. "I know what Tolly Shephard did and didn't do—and what they did to his son to gain his compliance when he played both sides. He's dead, but Gail isn't, and she still has to get up every morning and come to terms with all the secrets Tolly had. Mark, you've turned this island upside down and woken up a lot of people to what has been happening behind their backs. No one saw it. The town council is in a state of flux. You have interim appointees, as the mayor and councilors are now charged, awaiting trial. The entire CPS department has been turned upside down, and jobs are still being vacated. You're a hero for the children, Mark, but you have to know many of the island folks have turned on Gail. Their anger is misdirected. Her truck was spray painted with *CHILD KILLER*. People she's known forever on the island have phoned and said some horrible things…"

"Someone vandalized her truck?" he cut in. "Why didn't she call me? When did this happen?"

Billy Jo glanced over to the window. Her three-legged cat was curled up on the cat tree, whereas Lucky had padded into the kitchen and was lapping water out of his dog bowl. She started back toward him in the fuzzy robe that was more warm than flattering, and he didn't know what to make of the shadows around her eyes. He knew well the places her head went when she struggled. What she was thinking, he had no idea.

"Gail won't phone you," she said. "Not that she thinks

you wouldn't show up and file a report, because she knows you would, but I think she believes that because of what Tolly did, she deserves every hateful thing coming at her. Yet every time someone lashes out at her, it kills a little piece of her soul. I can see it. I know Tolly wasn't strong enough to end things the way you did. But I also know he hid it well. So tonight we'll take a pizza over, talk to her and be civilized, and let her know she's a human being and we care."

Maybe it was the way she'd said it, but he wondered whether she understood how he felt about Gail. He couldn't look at her without seeing Tolly.

Instead of saying something, he took another swallow of coffee.

"She thinks you hate her, Mark," Billy Jo said, striding back over to him. She put her mug down on the island, not looking away from what he knew was likely shock staring back at her.

"Excuse me?" he said. "I don't hate her. Where would she ever get an idea like that?"

Billy Jo took another step toward him, sliding her hand on the island to touch the file again, likely seeing the names listed. "Maybe it's because you make excuses never to go and see her. I show up alone, and every time I do, she asks about you, and I feel like I'm cheating when I say you're great but busy, or else you'd be there too. She doesn't believe one word of it, because she can see in my face that I'm lying. Or maybe it's because the last time she saw you was when you told her about Tolly."

Mark pulled his hand over his face, knowing she was right. He could feel the heavy sigh of frustration before it passed his lips.

"You going to make me go alone?" Billy Jo said, pulling her arms over her chest, not looking away.

"I don't hate her," he said. "I just don't know what to say to her. There's a difference."

Billy Jo glanced away, pulling in a deep breath. Then she lifted her gaze, which had softened just a bit. "Sometimes just being there is all that's needed. Don't say anything. Don't pretend. Just pick up a piece of pizza and eat. Can you do that?"

He'd never known Billy Jo to be so reasonable. "I can do that."

She ran her hand over his arm, rose up on her tiptoes, and kissed his cheek. "Good. And you may also want to consider asking Gail to help you dig into the people here. Pick her brain," she said as she reached for her mug and topped it with more coffee.

He wondered if she'd lost her mind. "Breaking bread with Gail is one thing, Billy Jo, but I'm not having her anywhere near this." He knew it had come out rather sharply. He had felt the bite in his words.

Billy Jo blew on the steaming coffee and took a swallow. "Well, that's too bad, because I'm sure she could fill in a lot of holes about a lot of people that you wouldn't otherwise know. And it may help her feel as if she's doing something to make up for what Tolly did. It's a helpless feeling, Mark, feeling responsible even though it's not logical. You could dig and miss something Gail knows that you would never have figured out in a million years. She's been here, like, forever." She tapped his arm again. "Think about it, Mark. That's all I ask."

Then she walked away, and he watched her, her heavy socks, her warm housecoat. This time, she didn't look back.

He reached for the file, seeing the names, as the shower popped on.

"Yeah, there's no way I'm asking Tolly Shephard's

widow for help when it comes to anyone on this island," he muttered. Lucky brushed his leg, then looked up at him and whined. "Now, don't go looking at me like that. We'll go see her, eat pizza, and then leave."

There it was again, that sinking feeling he got every time he thought of Gail. As he took in the open file and the notes that only scratched the surface, he couldn't help thinking Billy Jo was too often right. But he wouldn't ask Gail even though she could clear up a lot of questions about a lot of people.

No, involving Gail was exactly what he wasn't going to do.

Mark dropped the files on his desk just as Carmen walked into his office, wearing a dark blue sweater over blue jeans, dark hair pulled back in a ponytail. She was holding a file of her own, unsmiling, and her badge was pinned to the waistband of her jeans, her gun holstered.

She closed the door. "You know, there's a point where I wonder whether I'll go to hell," she said as she held out the file to Mark. "You have any idea how hard it was for me not to look at Lacy while I was digging into her personal life, learning the kinds of things I shouldn't and don't want to know? God damn, Chief, we all have something in our closets. Now I know way too much."

Mark reached for the file and glanced out of his glassed-in office to where Lacy was filling Lucky's dog dish with more kibble. Her hair was short, a mix of white and dark. The scent of fresh brewing coffee was a reminder he needed another cup. He set the file atop the others on his desk, then shrugged out of his jean jacket and tossed it on a hook on the spindly old coat tree that had come with the office. "Good morning to you, too," he said to Carmen, noting the impatience in her face and how stiffly she stood. "Any red flags? Anything stick out that I need to see?"

Carmen pulled her arms over her chest and made a rude noise as she shook her head. "Let's see. She's had a total of four different cell phones. Seems she cancels one when she gets a better deal somewhere else. Maybe I should ask her about that, considering my own carrier seems to be screwing me over and over. She has accounts at three different banks. The highest balance is with the local credit union, just over three thousand, give or take. The other two carry balances of only around fifty dollars.

"She's been divorced twice. Has a daughter who's married, living in New Mexico. Ex number one is the father. Looks like the scumbag drained their bank account and took out a second and third mortgage on the house they owned, then lost everything to gambling debts, drinking, and a fondness for cocaine. The only good thing he did for her was up and leave. Lacy and her daughter were on food stamps and welfare for six months.

"Then she worked a job in Astoria for three months before picking up odd jobs back on the island and living in an old travel trailer on the north end for a year. She worked at the cheese factory, one of the local farms, the brewery, and the grocery store, then cleaned houses and waited tables at four of the restaurants on the island. Deadbeat number two she married and divorced in six months. During that time, roughly ten years back, there was a complaint on file that Tolly responded to."

Mark opened the file, taking in the pages of notes. Hearing the name of the old chief, he was still having trouble coming to terms with his death. It sucker-punched him every time. Those last moments he had seen Tolly alive still haunted him.

"What kind of trouble was it?" he said, flipping the pages.

Carmen leaned on his desk and pointed to the third page, halfway down. "She pulled a shotgun on deadbeat number two and threw him out of the house, her house, which she bought after scraping together enough money. The deadbeat called Tolly, saying she was trying to kill him, which apparently was how Tolly found her when he arrived on scene. He took the shotgun and talked the deadbeat into leaving quietly. Looks like the deadbeat hired a lawyer to push it further, though, and ended up getting half of what Lacy had managed to put away. A nice fat payday. Evidently, he had taken up with Dori Little, who runs the post office, and it doesn't take a rocket scientist to figure out that Lacy busted him for the affair. Lacy had to move, because him taking half meant selling the only thing that was hers. That put her in the little house she now owns by the cove."

Mark flicked his gaze over to Carmen. He knew by the way she had hesitated that she wasn't done. He lifted a brow but said nothing, and she gestured toward the file again.

"If you're wondering whether Dori is still with the deadbeat, no. Seems she saw the light not long after. For the record, I can see why Lacy has decided men aren't worth the effort. She's remained single, and for that she's kept her house and her bank accounts." Carmen pulled in a heavy breath and tossed an uneasy glance over her shoulder. "Now how the hell am I supposed to look her in the eye, knowing what I know about her messy personal life? God dammit, Chief, if anyone looked into my past..." She angled her head. "Wait, you looked into my past?"

At the sharpness in her tone, he felt pinned by her scrutiny. He made himself clear his throat. "You were always a tough one to read. I looked into you long ago, Carmen. For the record, you were screwed over. Always bothered me what happened with your kid. But, cards on the table, I'm pretty sure you've done your own digging into my life, probably before I got here. So now that we all know everything about each other, let's move past it. Good to know there's nothing to worry about with Lacy and my instincts about her were right on."

There it was, the blank look Carmen had mastered. She blew out a breath. Maybe she was still stuck on the fact that he knew she was human just like he was. "Fine," was all she said, with a ton of snark. She glanced away just as there was a tap on the door and it popped open.

"Chief, coffee's ready," Lacy said, leaning in. "Lucky is out of kibble, so I'm going to make a quick run to the corner store."

Carmen was quiet, with an expression that gave nothing away. She pulled her arms over her chest, awkward.

"Oh, and are you done dissecting my past, Carmen?" Lacy continued. "Found all my skeletons? My bank called with one of those automated alerts, said someone had pulled my credit, which I thought was odd, since I'm not in the market to buy anything. I've learned the hard way from deadbeats trying to steal from me, so I know when someone is doing something they shouldn't behind my back. Then there was the fact that you couldn't look me in the eye for two days.

"Well, I'm not an idiot. I know you're looking into everyone on this island. Wondered when my turn was coming. Guess I have my answer. Yes, I'm not perfect. My credit is average. Never understood the world of finance, but I did figure out how to balance my own checkbook after living in a moldy trailer for a year with my daughter.

Never put all my money in one bank, either, and I've finally figured out how to stop paying endless fees. I've never stolen anything except for the candy I pocketed when I was five and my mother wasn't looking. My car I own outright, and I have no secret stash of cash anywhere. Wish I did. Oh, and I've been binge-watching Netflix before I cancel that subscription. I'm too cheap to purchase cable, and I have time on my hands since spring is coming and I'm waiting for the ground to thaw so I can expand my garden. Any other questions?"

Carmen appeared uncomfortable in the face of Lacy's calm. Damn, he really liked her.

"Just one candy?" Mark said as he closed Lacy's file.

A twitch of a smile pulled at the edges of her lips. She only shook her head.

"Thanks, Lacy," he said. "Appreciate it, you taking care of my dog." He pulled a twenty from his wallet and held it out to her, and she walked around Carmen, saying nothing. The icy chill that lingered had him wincing.

"Oh, and, Chief," Lacy said as she took the twenty, "you may want to stop in and have a word with Shana Guzman. She owns the local pub, the Dog and Whistle. She mentioned last night that her ex surprised the hell out of her by moving here after she hadn't heard from him in, like, forever. She was downright pissed, too. Apparently, he said something about wanting to make amends."

Mark dragged his gaze to Carmen, who had an odd expression—curiosity or pensiveness, he wasn't sure. "Shana and her ex, what do we know about them?" he said.

Carmen lifted her hands. "I know nothing about him. Shana has a kid, I think…"

"Shana grew up here," Lacy said. "Nice lady. Locals know her. She's a straight shooter but, like many of us, attracts the wrong kind. She's always been hard working. Hasn't heard from her ex since her daughter was two. Just saying, because I know you want to know about everyone on the island, he apparently bought forty acres on the west side. Showed up the other day, and I've never seen Shana so angry. All I know is she doesn't trust him." Lacy stepped back. "You'll listen for the phone?"

"Yeah, we got it," Mark said, and Lacy was already walking back to her desk.

"You want me to take that one, add it to the list?" Carmen said.

Mark watched Lacy grab her purse and head out. It was suddenly so quiet, and that sinking feeling he had too often was back. "Nope, I've got this one. You just keep working through everyone in town." The coffee smelled tempting, but the knot in his stomach and the tightness that pulled across his shoulders had him glancing at the clock on the wall and reaching for his jacket on the coat tree. "I'm going to have a word with Shana, find out who this ex is. You hold down the fort and try to smooth things over with Lacy."

"What do you want me to say?" Carmen said. "You're the one who told me to check into her, yet she's pissed at me."

Mark knew he had winced. He'd never understood why women were harder on other women than on men. "You want me to talk to her?"

Carmen uncrossed her arms and flicked her hand at him, giving him the pissed-off vibe that seemed to roll off her at times. "I don't need anyone running interference for me," she said, then walked out of his office past Lucky, who was walking in.

Mark considered this for only a second before reaching for his keys and saying, "Come on, boy, let's go."

Mark could feel the rain in the air as he stepped out of his Jeep into the parking lot, empty except for an older green Subaru.

"Come on, boy," he said, then waited for Lucky to jump down before he closed the door.

His cowboy boots scraped the gravel as he took in the old clapboard building, painted a light tan, and the old neon sign for the Dog and Whistle, which had wires sticking out, wrapped in electrical tape. There were beer bottles on the railing of the old porch.

He pulled open the door and heard the clink of glasses. The scent of stale beer hit him as he pulled off his sunglasses and tucked them in his shirtfront.

"I'm closed. Don't open until eleven," Shana called out with her back to him, her dark hair pulled into a ponytail, carrying a handful of dirty glasses. Then she turned around.

"I can see that," he said. "Hoping to have a word or two with you, Shana."

She set the glasses on a tray, then reached for a gray

dish bin and headed toward a table still covered with dirty glasses. She was a short woman, not much taller than Billy Jo, with a round face. He figured she was in her late thirties, give or take. "You want a word with me, Chief? What about? Something happen I need to worry about? Can tell you it was a quiet night yesterday aside from a few of the usual rowdies, who otherwise behaved themselves."

Mark took in the tables, the old wood chairs, and a pool table at the far end.

"Your dog going to behave himself too?" Shana said, her gaze going right to Lucky. "I just mopped the floor and don't intend to wash it again." She jutted her chin to a bucket and mop in the corner.

"Don't worry about him," he said.

"Mm-hmm," was all she said in response.

"Lacy said something about your ex moving back here?"

Shana shook her head, clearing off the table, and reached for the bar towel over the shoulder of her black t-shirt. When she straightened, wiping her hands, she gave him a scowl he hadn't expected. "Walter? You want to talk to me about Walter? What the hell did he do? What is this really about?" She tossed the towel back over her shoulder and lifted her hands, oozing tension. Evidently, there was more than a story here.

"You know we've had some trouble on the island," he said. "Just doing my due diligence when I heard he recently moved back. You've had problems with him?"

She shook her head and frowned before letting out a rough laugh. "Problems? The man did me a favor by walking out on us without a word when Haley, my daughter, was two. At the time, he didn't give me the time of day or return one call. Now he suddenly shows up and says he wants to make amends after basically telling me to go fuck myself without saying a word? I'm pissed that he thinks he can just walk back into my life, my daughter's life. He bought a place, not just any place but a nice piece of property, forty acres, a nice big house, yet he couldn't give two cents to his kid? No, no problems. I'm totally peachy," she said with a bite.

Mark never had been able to navigate women's emotions. "Didn't know that," he said. "An expensive property? So he's worth something."

Shana made a rude noise as she lifted the gray bin, glasses clinking, and walked back around the bar. "Guess that all depends on how you define being worth something."

Mark walked over to the bar and gestured to Lucky to sit. "You have any idea why he suddenly moved here?"

Shana was now wiping down the bar again, her face not hiding her dislike. "No idea. As I said, he showed up here, walked in after years without a word, and said he wanted to make things right. I told him to go fuck himself. He asked me to hear him out, said he had reasons for doing what he did. I told him at one time I might have listened, but I really don't give a shit now. As a matter of fact, I told him to leave and not set foot back in my bar." She pointed to the bar top before picking up the rag again and scrubbing at it. "This is my place. Now, why he's here is the million-dollar question. I really don't care, but if he has any ideas about inserting himself into Haley's life or mine, he won't get that chance, and I told him as much. But you haven't told me what he's done or why you're asking about him." She had finally stopped wiping the scratched dark brown bar counter and looked up at him, unsmiling.

"Just doing my due diligence, Shana. I don't have anything on him. Lacy mentioned him to me this morning, and I just want to make sure everything is on the up and up, that he's not moving here to cause problems. Is he retired, working? I mean, what does he do?"

Shana glanced away and then smiled. "Ah, Lacy. Love her. Didn't expect her to go to you. You planning on paying him a visit? Maybe you can ask him all that, because me asking would mean I give a shit, and I don't. And, while you're at it, remind him of the fact that he walked out of our lives, so he should stay out."

Now he had more questions.

"Well, you're my first stop, and he's my next," he said. "I'll be sure to ask him. So what can you tell me about him, Walter Guzman?"

"Crandall," she said. "His name is Walter Crandall. I kept my name, and in fact, my daughter has my name too. Of every bad choice I made, giving her his name was not one, though I've had no shortage of people forcing their opinions on me about how not okay that was. As far as I know, he's never been in trouble with the law. He never cheated on me, either, as far as I know. Instead, he worked all the time. Yes, his first love was his career, and I was second. He has a fondness for vanilla ice cream, hates seafood. Used to run in his younger days, but only when he was stressed. He doesn't much care for animals, would never allow me to get a cat or dog. He's a neat freak, can't stand dirt, to the point that a glass can't even be left in the sink. He has a thing for shoes. Hates beer but has a fondness for chocolate-flavored whiskey. He wouldn't be caught dead in a place like this. Hates most sports except cricket."

Mark was getting a picture of someone he didn't see fitting in on the island. Maybe his expression said so, as an odd smile pulled at the corners of Shana's lips.

"Wondering how someone like me could end up with someone like that?" she said.

He had to remind himself he hadn't yet met this man, but the image she had painted wasn't flattering. He made himself shake his head. "I'm not going there. So, as far as you know, he's not involved in anything questionable?"

"Define questionable." She leaned on the bar, her brows raised, her gaze intense.

"Anything that raises a red flag."

She leaned back. "You'll have to ask him, because even now, I'm wondering how I could have ever fallen for him. The best thing that came out of our being together was my daughter, and the next was him leaving. Other than that…" She lifted her hands and gave her head another shake. "Seriously, I have no idea why he's here. I didn't ask. Red flags? I don't know. He works all the time. When he wasn't working, he was always thinking of work. Anything else?"

The way she'd said it, he realized she really didn't want to know. That was something else he hadn't expected.

"What does he do for work?" he said.

She pulled in a breath. "He's a corporate executive. Marketing, that kind of thing. On a big scale, though. He runs a department for a big company, with a sizable staff working under him. He was always giving presentations, putting together sales pitches, closing deals. Nothing that interests me in the least. Are you looking for his specific job duties? That's not something we discussed, ever, because I have no interest. All I know is he works with the kind of people I'm not interested in meeting, the kind of people who don't bat an eye at paying a thousand dollars for dinner. I didn't attend anything with him after we were married. At the time, I told myself it was because he knew I wasn't interested, wouldn't know the difference between a butter knife and a table knife, and failed miserably at bull-shit small talk. He found it amusing. Whatever events he went to, he went alone. But in hindsight, I often wonder why he was so willing to keep me out of it."

He just stared at her, again wondering why that unsettled feeling just wouldn't go away. Her gaze seemed to soften, and he wasn't sure what she was thinking as she let out a sigh.

"Yeah, we really weren't a match," she said. "Sorry, Chief, that's all I can tell you. Again, as to why he's really here, your guess is as good as mine."

"Thanks, Shana," Mark said. "Anything else? Oh, and do you have his address, by any chance?"

She turned and reached into a box behind the bar to pull out a card. "I can do better than that. He left his card with a phone number and address." She held it out to him, and Mark reached for it.

"I can take a photo with my phone," he said, but she only waved him off.

"Keep it, really. He left it on the bar, and instead of tossing it, I kept it. Seriously, you'll be doing me a favor."

Mark shoved the card with the address scribbled on the back in his jacket pocket, then started to the door, saying, "Come on, Lucky."

"Oh, and, Chief, one more thing," Shana called out.

He turned back to her, his hand already on the door.

"When you see Walter, give him a message for me. Tell him Haley and I are doing fine, better than fine, and if he gives a shit about his daughter, he'll stay away from us. She doesn't need him walking back into her life now to mess things up. And as far as making things right, tell him I'm not interested."

He didn't know what to say, taking in the sharpness in her gaze. "I'll give him your message. Thanks again, Shana," he said. Then he walked out the door, his dog following him.

He felt the rain sprinkling down as he pulled open the door to the Jeep and said, "Get in there, boy." As Lucky jumped in, he took another second to observe the old bar, which wasn't much to look at, and he wondered what kinds of things his digging would turn up on Walter Crandall.

A man who wanted to make amends was someone who'd done something he needed to make amends for. Was it just the fact that he'd walked out on a wife and kid?

Mark climbed in his Jeep and started the engine. Running his hand over his dog in the passenger seat, he took in the old car he knew belonged to Shana. Something about all of this just didn't sit right.

CHAPTER

Four

Billy Jo's windshield wipers flicked back and forth in the light rain as she pulled down a paved circular driveway bordered by trees and bushes, taking in the gloom and dreariness that seemed to affect more people than not on the island. The once landscaped front yard, always neat and tidy, was now piled with old wet leaves and debris that appeared forgotten.

As she pulled up in front of Gail's house, the siding that she thought had been white seemed mostly filled with hints of gray. So much had changed, as if the life of the home were slowly seeping away. It was just a feeling she got. Something about this house, this once welcoming property, seemed so empty. Loss hung heavy in the air.

Gail's pickup was parked in front of an older tan Explorer she knew had to be Tolly's, with a bad paint job she knew was to cover up the vandalism. She put her car in park and turned off the engine, breathing in the large shrimp and mushroom pizza, which she knew was Gail's favorite. Damn, she wished she could do more for her.

She reached for her cell phone and saw nothing from

Mark, a silence she hoped wasn't his way of saying he wouldn't show. There were times she wanted to wring his neck. She typed out a quick text: *Where are you? I'm at Gail's and you're not! Don't you dare not show.*

She waited for a moment, feeling the knot in her stomach before she saw the three dots and then his text back: *On my way. Do you need me to pick up pizza?*

She let out a breath. The front door had opened, and Gail was standing there, her arms crossed. Damn, she looked as if she'd lost more weight. She didn't smile but lifted her hand in a wave.

Billy Jo sent off a reply. *No, I already did. Just hurry your ass up before it gets cold.*

His message popped up again: *Five minutes, promise.*

Billy Jo shoved her phone in her purse, reached for the pizza box, and climbed out, juggling the box as she lifted her bulky purse over her shoulder. "Hi, Gail. Mark's on his way," she said.

Just then, she heard his Jeep and spotted him driving in fast, the way he always did. He parked behind her as she shoved her door closed, and she waited as he climbed out and held the door for Lucky to jump down, his tail wagging all the way over to her.

"Hey, you." She gave him a rub with her free hand, and then he took off to Gail as Mark strode over to her. "You made it," she couldn't help herself from saying.

He lifted his hand and called out, "Hey, Gail!" before he reached for the pizza box, then leaned in and kissed her.

"How was your day?" she said, not knowing what to make of his blue eyes. Something was on his mind, or maybe whatever emotion she saw there was because she was making him break bread with Gail. She knew how much trouble he was having with all of this. She reached over and touched his arm, feeling his heavy jean jacket. The rain was beginning to pick up a bit.

"Fine, busy," he said. "Some crazy stuff and more crap. How was yours? Thought you were going to drop by the station first?" He managed to turn her and slide his hand over her lower back to have them walking to the open door, which Lucky had already gone through.

"Couldn't because my day got away from me." And the pizza place was closer to Gail's than town. "I sent you a text."

Mark said nothing at the same time Billy Jo didn't miss the shadows that filled Gail's eyes as she stared at Mark, not trying to force a smile, and said, "How have you been?"

The edge in her tone gave away how much she was struggling. A good day, a bad day? Billy Jo figured the latter, by the gray sweats and bulky beige sweater, which she was pretty sure was Tolly's.

"I'm good, Gail," Mark said. "See you have some yard work that needs taking care of."

Gail didn't pull her gaze from Mark. The fondness that had always been there between them was now a wariness. "Had other things on my mind," she said, and there it was, an awkwardness that lingered. Billy Jo had to fight the urge to wince.

"Well, I don't know about you two, but I'm absolutely starving," she said. "I see Lucky has already made himself at home."

Gail stepped back. "Come on in, you two. Sorry this is still kind of awkward. I don't have many stopping by. It's been quite a while, Mark."

Billy Jo kicked off her shoes, and Mark closed the door behind him and gave his cowboy boots a quick wipe but kept them on.

"Well, can I get either of you a beer?" Gail said. "I don't have any wine left and haven't worked up enough nerve to go into town. Plan on making another trip off island to stock up on things." She had walked on ahead into the kitchen.

Billy Jo tapped Mark on the chest and looked up to him, making a face.

"What?" he said in a low voice. "I'm here, aren't I?"

She only shook her head as she walked ahead of him, and Mark called out, "Beer sounds good, Gail."

Gail had filled a bowl with water and set it on the floor, and Lucky was already lapping it up. Billy Jo took in the counter, which was filled with empty bottles: wine, beer, a few liquors. In the family room, boxes were stacked in the corner, and in the fireplace she could see half-burned paper. She made herself look over at Gail. "Never been a beer drinker," she said. "I'll just have some water."

Gail pulled a beer from the fridge and held it out to Mark, saying, "Here you go."

"Thanks, Gail." Mark twisted off the cap.

Billy Jo listened to Lucky lapping up the water as she shrugged out of her dark blue jacket and set it over the back of the chair. Mark had settled the pizza box on the counter. She realized Gail was already drinking a beer, evidently having started before they came. She was distracted, carrying the weight of everything on her shoulders. She'd already forgotten about Billy Jo's water.

"Let me get some plates," she said.

Damn, this was awkward. Maybe she should have come alone. She glanced over to Mark, who was looking around, staring at the boxes. He took a swallow of beer and shot her a look, having picked up on the problem. Billy Jo listened to the clatter as Gail set the plates down along with a roll of paper towels, then lifted the box lid.

"Mark, come on," she said. "I know you never shy away from eating. Dig in, considering you brought the pizza."

Billy Jo didn't wait. She dropped a piece of pizza on a plate and handed it to Mark, and his blue eyes didn't pull away. He really was struggling with being there. What was it with guys? She supposed Mark never got into an emotional black hole when he was struggling. She dropped another piece on a second plate and said, "Here, Gail," then waited for Gail to take it before getting a piece for herself.

Mark sat at the head of the table with a scrape of his chair, Gail at the other end, and Billy Jo took a bite of the pizza before she walked over to the cupboard and pulled out a glass.

"Oh, geez, Billy Jo, I forgot about your water," Gail said, scooting back her chair to get up.

"Don't worry, I got it," Billy Jo said. "Sit down, Gail." She filled the glass from the tap, brought it and her plate to the table, and fetched the box from the island as well before sitting down at the empty chair in the middle.

Mark shoved the last of his piece in his mouth and reached for another. Gail took the tiniest bite ever and kept looking awkwardly over to Mark. Damn, the silence was unnerving.

"So what's with the empty bottles?" Billy Jo said after taking another bite. "You been drinking alone or cleaning house?"

Gail dropped her half-eaten pizza on her plate and wiped her hands together before leaning back, reaching for her beer, and tipping it to drink. She looked over to Billy Jo, gesturing with the beer in her hand as she said, "Cleaning up, you could say. Those are from a while ago. Knowing you were coming, the place was…well, let's just say I'm not much of a cleaner lately. It was so bad that I realized I needed to at least run the vacuum. But once I started vacuuming, I had to pick up, and one thing led to another…" Gail took another swallow of her beer and finished it.

Billy Jo couldn't help wondering how much she'd been drinking. She took in the short haircut she was sporting and the dark circles that had appeared under her eyes since Mark had told her about Tolly. "You sleeping?" she asked.

Gail shrugged.

Mark had finished off another piece and reached for a third, but this time he shot a quick glance to Billy Jo and then to Gail, and she realized he was listening more than she'd realized.

"Is that a yes or a no?" she said. "I see you've lost more weight, too."

Gail let out a heavy sigh and a rough laugh. "Yes, Mom, the nights suck because that's when the ghosts come out." She reached for her pizza again and made herself take a bite. "I'm sleeping a few hours at a time. Had a nap before you came, so there is that. But I'd rather talk about anything else. You two, you look happy, good. Tell me what's going on with you, the new house, anything. Come on, I need a distraction."

Billy Jo had to fight the urge to redirect the conversation back and make her talk about the ghosts, her feelings, and how she was really doing.

"I'm investigating everyone on the island," Mark said, leaning back in his chair with a creak. He took another bite and chewed, then swallowed, and his heavy gaze connected with hers. She felt every day that they were more and more on the same page, but then there was this.

"You're investigating everyone? Why? For what?" Gail leaned on the table, her pizza back on her plate.

"We had a den of pedophiles here in positions of power, and the entire time I've been on this island, there has been one bad actor after another. It seems the elite of the world use this place as their personal playground. I'm looking into everyone. I want to know why everyone is here, how they make their money, and any secrets they're hiding. Everyone has them, so I'm going to do my due diligence and find out what everyone is about, one by one. I will look into everyone's closet so that never again will shenanigans of any kind happen on this island."

Mark hadn't pulled his gaze from Gail. For a moment, Billy Jo couldn't wrap her head around what he was doing, bringing up the very thing he'd said he didn't want Gail anywhere near.

"You're investigating people who haven't done anything?" Gail said. "Kind of stepping over the line there, Mark." She put her pizza down and brushed her hands together. "But I have to say I agree with you."

Billy Jo turned to Gail, taking in the awkwardness and a hint of something she hadn't seen in a long time. She wondered sometimes about the shadows that haunted her still. When would Tolly and what he'd done, what he'd been part of, leave her?

Gail glanced out the window and then back to Mark. "Can I help?"

Billy Jo turned to Mark, she was still holding her pizza. Mark was considering as he finished chewing, wearing that look he had when he was focused, saying nothing. She dragged her gaze back over to Gail, who was watching Mark expectantly. For a moment, she wanted to kick him under the table.

"Yeah, actually, you can," he said.

Billy Jo whipped her head back to him. This had been

her idea, and he'd said hell no. He must have realized she was staring at him, but he didn't look her way.

"Wonderful," Gail said. "How?"

Billy Jo angled her head, and now Mark did glance her way.

"What can you tell me about Shana Guzman, who owns the Dog and Whistle, and her ex, Walter Crandall, who just moved back to the island?" he said. "She hates him. He disappeared for a while and now wants to make amends, though I don't know for what, exactly." He moved in the wooden chair, and it creaked again as he leaned back, setting a hand on the table. "Let's start there. Tell me everything you know about both of them—who he is, what he does, and any ideas you have about why he's suddenly back on the island. I want to know what he did and for whom, because I have to tell you, something about this and him isn't sitting right."

Mark had that look about him again. Billy Jo didn't know who the hell he was talking about, but he glanced back over to her as he said, "I get a feeling when something is off, and I have it now. Walter Crandall and Shana Guzman, I want to know everything about their story and what, exactly, he's hiding in his closet."

CHAPTER
Five

Billy Jo had a way of watching him that felt as if she were shooting daggers his way. She was intense, bold, and he couldn't pull anything on her. He knew he should have talked to her before bringing up Shana and her ex, because Billy Jo and surprises couldn't coexist. In fact, she was likely to pull him out of the room soon and ask him what the fuck he was doing.

But instead of letting her, he leaned forward and set his hand over hers, and she stiffened. She settled down only when she was damn good and ready. Then there was Gail, who had seemed to brighten from the sadness and despair that was sucking the very life out of her.

"Sorry, babe," Mark said. "I know I should have mentioned this. Just been a shitty day. Never know what's going to come out of left field. Gail, you should know that my wife suggested I ask you to lend a hand and give your insight into the people here, and I think she's right. I mean, you know the people on this island better than I do, better than most, and could likely save me a lot of time and digging."

Gail leaned back, having suddenly gone quiet, and he didn't know what to make of the expression on her face. "You know, Mark, I do know the people on this island, but some of the people I thought I knew, I realized I didn't know them at all. You're right about one thing: People can hide horrible secrets, and what you see isn't always what's real."

Now he knew she was talking about the preacher and Tolly. He wondered if he'd ever get the image of the last moments of Tolly's life out of his head. He knew Billy Jo was right; he was going to have to sit down and talk with Gail about Tolly, only he didn't know if he'd ever be able to find the words.

"Yes, that's true about everyone, Gail," Billy Jo said, "but you know people here, and I think you can help make it easier for Mark so he's not starting from scratch when he's looking into them. This island has a lot of people who own places here but live elsewhere. You know who parks their money in real estate, who visits maybe a few weeks a year, and who lives here full time, and you know who the original residents of the island are. I bet you know a lot of secrets Mark doesn't."

Mark hadn't expected this reasonable encouragement from Billy Jo, who had pulled her hand out from under his and leaned back, crossing her arms over her chest. At times, she was so damn hard to read, and he knew he had to tread carefully.

"Did you have any idea of the wise woman you were marrying, Mark?" Gail said.

He had to remind himself every day. "I know how lucky I am," he replied.

Billy Jo didn't look at him right away, but when she did, that familiar awkwardness was there. She still didn't know how to take a compliment. Gail was watching them both closely, and Billy Jo didn't appear amused.

"Okay, so Shana and Walter," Mark said, then sighed and leaned forward, resting his forearms on the table after he had pushed his plate away. He reached for his beer and took a swallow. Billy Jo was still watching him, and he knew she wanted a word or two with him.

"Shana is a damn hard worker," Gail said. "She and Walter were never a match. You know how some men marry beneath them? Well, Walter comes from that world. With his people, with the circles he moved in, Shana never fit. I have no idea how they met, but I do know Shana is one of the island kids. She grew up with backwoods bonfires, swimming at the local lakes, roasting hotdogs over a fire, and crushing peanuts on the floor of the old bar, whereas Walter is all about black tie events, Gucci, and getting a reservation at a five-star restaurant where the dinner service placement confuses the hell out of the average person. Shana wouldn't have a clue which fork to use, or which knife, or that the drinkware depends on the wine you choose. Don't even get me started on the bread plate and whether it goes on the right or left. The types of formal dinners Walter was accustomed to have a dress code, jacket and tie or dress and heels, with butlers and etiquette to boot.

"I remember hearing from her once what a nightmare it was the one time he took her to a charity dinner, a work dinner. She was expecting something resembling what you might see with a local charity, maybe auctions or something with the money going to the needy. After all, what is a charity for? But she was humiliated when she discovered the dinner was only about getting money for a large foundation. She never really understood the people there, who she never in a million years could have fit in with. She said everything about the night was all show. She messed up every protocol possible, using the wrong fork, taking bread from the plate of the man to her right, not having a clue what the hell anyone was talking about. She drank too much and spilled her last glass of wine.

"That was all she shared. She was embarrassed and uncomfortable, and she said Walter was furious with her. When they got home, she told him not to ever take her to an event like that again. Apparently, he didn't. He went alone, and she worked at her bar, and eventually he went off island to wherever he went. Never saw them together at all. I do know he worked for some big philanthropic foundation, and when I say big, I mean big, all about money. The people he worked with lived in a world the average person is never invited to.

"Shana didn't want any part of it. What exactly he did I can't tell you, but I do know he worked with private family foundations, handling the kind of money you and I will never see in this lifetime. To tell you the truth, it's not so much that he and Shana were opposites, because opposites do work at times. It was that Shana didn't belong in his world. Anyway, he was always away, traveling for work, I suppose, and it wasn't as if they had been together that long. Don't know why he married her—on a whim, maybe. But then she was pregnant, and if I recall, he wasn't even in town when his daughter was born." She pulled her arms across her chest, and her brow knit. She was thinking.

"Shana said he walked out when her daughter was two," Mark said. "He didn't provide any support, just left."

Gail shrugged. "I don't know about that, but I heard that one day he was there and the next he was gone. Shana kept her head up and moved on. News came that they divorced, but she didn't share much about it. You said Walter has moved back to the island?"

Mark didn't have to look over to his wife to know she was still watching him closely. He tapped the table. "Yes. I stopped in and had a word with Shana. He bought a big property on the west end."

"You mean the forty waterfront acres with the boat house and caretaker's house?" Gail said. "It's a gated property that was listed at twelve million and change."

He really didn't know the island like Gail. Now he did glance at Billy Jo. "Well, I didn't have a chance to check that part, but it sounds about right. Take it you know the property? I had Carmen run the address and tax records. Haven't paid him a visit yet, but I plan to after I run a few checks on him first."

Billy Jo had looked away and become unusually quiet.

"Where would you look first?" Mark said, flicking his gaze to Gail, who looked between Billy Jo and him.

"Well, I would find out why he's here," she said. "Go talk to him face to face and get a read on him before you start digging into his past, his life. Come on, Mark. You have the best instincts in a cop, and you know when someone's lying to you or something is off. But at the same time, and this is just a word of advice, you also want to be careful how much you dig, because the kind of investigating you're doing could lead you down rabbit holes you may not want to go down. Everyone has secrets, things they'd never want anyone to know about them. And sometimes those secrets can be dark and dirty, and they change how people see you in the community. If he's a bad guy, sure, you expose the shit out of him. But if you're not one hundred percent sure, remember that in the wrong hands, a well-placed lie or assumption can spread like wildfire. And that can destroy someone."

He wondered whether they were talking about her now, about how the people of the island had tarred and feathered her over what Tolly had done. Billy Jo still said nothing.

"I know very well how misinformation and disinformation are used," Mark said, "and I'm also well aware of how to destroy someone's credibility with a well-placed and believable lie. You probably know who on the island is trustworthy, who is questionable, who not to trust, and who looks too good to be true."

The quiet was unsettling. Gail flicked her blue eyes, which were filled with the weight of the world, over to him as she said, "So how does this work? You want to call me or just swing by when you have questions?"

Billy Jo pulled in a rather deep breath. "How it works is that you'll need to leave this house, Gail. You'll work out of the station," she said, then turned her sharp gaze on Mark, who knew he was frowning. "That works for you, doesn't it, Mark?"

Now what the hell was he supposed to say? He tapped his fingers on the table and took in the tightness around his wife's mouth.

"Sure," was all he said, though he suspected that having Gail work out of the station was not a good idea at all.

"What the hell was that about?" Mark shouted, slamming the front door shut.

Billy Jo, still in her coat, was filling a bowl of soft food for Harley, who meowed as he hopped on three legs over to her. She heard Mark's footsteps and Lucky's nails on the hardwood, and she turned to take in the man she had married, who was now standing on the other side of the island, in his jean jacket, with an expression that said he was ready to argue.

"You're going to have to be a little more specific, Mark," she said, keeping her voice calm.

He angled his head and opened his mouth as if he were at a loss for words, then made a rude noise before pulling his hand over his face and giving a rough laugh. She knew she could push him only so far. "Specifically?" he said. "Really, is that what we're doing? You put me in the sudden position of having Gail working back at the station, the police station, where she can't be because the people of the island will have an absolute shitfit. It's one thing for me to pick her brain, to call her and go see her, but another for her to be in the sheriff's office again. You have any idea of the shit that will hit the fan? It won't be brows raised or questions; it will be pitchforks and torches, demands. No one will stop for a second to consider truth or reason. No matter what I say, they will not listen."

He lifted his hand before she could say anything. "And don't start about how people will see the whole picture, realize she's a victim, and not paint her with the same brush as Tolly. Because people will not. They believe what they believe because it fits their narrative. No matter how much I try to convince people to be open and see past their horror and beliefs, the truth will not change their minds. We aren't even close to being there. And should we talk about how you were out the door well before me, without so much as a 'See you at home,' driving so fast I was tempted to pull you over and give you a ticket?" He was now pacing.

Harley meowed again, so Billy Jo set a bowl of kibble down beside his water as well. Seeing Lucky eyeing the dish, she pulled open the island drawer and reached for a clean bowl and the container of dog food. Mark hadn't pulled his gaze from her, his vivid blue eyes flickering with a simmering fire.

"You were going to give me a ticket?" she said. "Are you planning on sleeping on the sofa?" She shrugged and placed both hands on the island. Lucky whined and then barked. "Okay, okay," she said to the dog as she filled his bowl and put it down on the floor not far from Harley.

Mark was shaking his head and pulling his hand over the back of his neck. "Bad choice of words," he said. "No, of course not. But it sure as shit looked as if you couldn't get away from me fast enough. I know when you're pissed, so just slow down. Why did you put me in that position,

Billy Jo?" His voice was low, and there was an edge to it. He let out a sigh.

"Why didn't you tell me first about Walter and Shana?" she replied. "You know it doesn't work for me, being out of the loop."

Mark shrugged out of his jean jacket and tossed it over the back of the kitchen chair, pacing in a circle. So he really wanted to get into it. "That's what this is about?" he said. "Well, sorry, babe, but I had a shitty day, putting out one fire after another, and didn't have time to stop and tell you before I had to show up at Gail's because you wanted me there. And maybe I was a little on edge because I had no idea she was as messed up as she was. Sorry I just blurted it out. I see my mistake now. She looks like shit, Billy Jo. How long has she been like that?"

Billy Jo let out a sigh. "You remember the day you told her about Tolly? I'll never forget your face, Mark, how upset you were. She hasn't gotten over it. That isn't the kind of news you can hear and then just get up the next day as if everything is okay. The fact is that the man she was married to was hiding something hideous. The people on the island haven't been too friendly to her, but nothing they've said has been worse than what she's thought about herself. I've heard it even from Pam: How could she not have known what Tolly was doing? But she can't hide her shellshock, and you have no idea how many times she's second-guessed everything, asking herself how she didn't see it. I know parents keep their kids away from her now, too. The whispers are horrible. She's been told on numerous occasions to leave the island. She's grieving, Mark. She now hates a man she loved deeply—or I don't know if she hates him. It's such a fine line between love and hate. I'm sorry to drop this on you. I realize I should have pulled you aside, I guess. Sorry, but you have avoided her."

He twisted his lips. The argument that had been simmering was now gone, and he shook his head and reached to pull his holstered gun off and set it on the counter. "I can't have her coming into the office," he said.

"Why not, Mark? Seriously, who cares what anyone thinks?"

"It's not that simple, Billy Jo. I'm the chief here, and I care about the reactions of people who still haven't come to grips with the fact that child traffickers have been using this island as their personal playground right under our noses. The former chief of police was tied to it, along with a priest, a cop, a few on the council, and how many others? Then there's the question of how Carmen and Lacy will take this."

Billy Jo fisted her hands. The isolation was the worst for Gail. "I know I'm asking a lot, Mark, but I'm afraid one day that I'm going to go over there and find that she's killed herself. She's alone. I don't even think her kids have come by to see her. She won't talk about them. I think even her family here are keeping their distance. She's in that house, seeing Tolly's things, drinking, not sleeping. That's a recipe for her not to wake up one day because she's downed a bottle of pills or taken one of Tolly's guns, put it to her head, and pulled the trigger. She has to get out of the house, do something to make things right even though she isn't responsible. I know it will make your job harder…"

He gave her a look and made a rude sound. "You're kidding, right? Harder? It will make it damn near impossible."

Billy Jo didn't say anything else. She knew when Mark was struggling with something.

He glanced away and reached for the holstered gun on the counter, then flicked those amazing blue eyes back to her. "You really think this will help her?" he said.

She nodded. "I do, Mark. Please do this for me. Gail isn't the evildoer here. Maybe you should lead the people by example."

He shook his head again, really struggling. "Fine," he said rather sharply. "I guess I'd better get ahead of this. I'll talk to the council in the morning, and to Carmen and Lacy. Then I need to drive over to this Walter Crandall's place and pay him a visit, have a word with him."

"About that," she said. "So you haven't met him yet? You said Lacy knows him? I've met Shana a few times. She seems nice. I didn't know anything about an ex."

Mark rested his hand over his gun. She knew he still needed to put it away. "No," he said. "Was halfway out to his place when I got called back, a disturbance I had to take care of. But I'm telling you, Billy Jo, something about this guy doesn't sit right. And yeah, Lacy mentioned him. She's friends with Shana. I did stop in to see her at her bar, cleaning up. She really has no use for the guy, and if he's worth what Gail said, then I can't figure out what he's doing back here. Shana said he wanted to make amends after walking out on his kid and her…"

"Maybe he woke up and wants to make right his mistake. Sometimes it can be that simple," Billy Jo cut in.

Mark shrugged. "Sure, anywhere else, but not here. I don't know, Billy Jo. It just seems as if this island has too many secrets. For some reason, this place is like a fucking magnet to the elites, like they tell each other to come on over and do whatever the hell they want here." His words dripped with sarcasm.

She only angled her head, because Mark was heading fast down a path of seeing only darkness and lies and evil.

She wondered if he'd ever be able to give anyone the benefit of the doubt again.

"You know what?" he said. "I'm going to grab a shower. You coming?"

Billy Jo closed the lid of Lucky's kibble. "You go ahead and get it warmed up. I'll be right there." She was starting to realize when he needed her to keep him anchored. He had started walking to the bedroom, his holstered pistol in his hand. "Hey, Mark, you mind if I tag along with you tomorrow when you go to see Walter Crandall?"

He stopped in the doorway and turned back to her, angling his head. "You want to come with me? Why?" He narrowed his gaze, suspicious, overthinking, as if always working on a puzzle in his mind.

She closed the cupboard and shrugged out of her coat, which she tossed over Mark's jean jacket on the wooden kitchen chair. Her husband was rather calm as he waited for her. "I don't know," she said. "Maybe your paranoia's rubbing off on me. I'm curious, have my own questions, maybe just want to hear his explanation. You have an idea when someone is lying to you, and so do I."

He lifted a brow and seemed to consider it for a second. "What about work?"

"I'll go in later."

He tapped the wood bedroom door frame. "Fine. First thing, we'll go pay him a visit. I've got to put this away." He gestured to the gun and walked into the bedroom.

She listened to him pulling open the closet and the familiar click of the gun safe. When she stopped in the doorway, his back was to her as he closed the closet. He had the most amazing wide shoulders, exuding strength. Damn, he was really something to look at. She loved him so much. When he pulled off his t-shirt, she took in the pale skin on his arm where a tattoo had once been.

"You okay?" he said as he walked into the bathroom, looking back from the doorway, lingering a second.

"Yeah, fine. I'm right behind you," she called out, but as the shower popped on, unease suddenly knotted in her chest, because for the first time, she realized she needed to be his backup. "I've got your back, Mark," she said quietly, then pulled off her clothes, tossed them into the hamper, and strode barefoot into the bathroom, taking in the steam from the glassed-in shower and the man she loved, her husband, waiting for her.

Billy Jo was really dragging again this morning, Mark thought as he filled two go-mugs with coffee after dumping his empty granola bowl in the dishwasher. His jean jacket was on and his gun holstered as he waited for her. Once again, she had been fast asleep when he woke up.

She strode out of the bedroom, yawning as she pulled a brush through her hair, wearing black jeans and a deep purple sweater.

"You sure you still want to come?" he said, holding the go mug out to her.

"Oh, this smells good. Thank you." She took a swallow, and he noticed dark circles under her eyes that hadn't been there the day before. "Yes, I'm coming. Thanks for waiting."

What was he supposed to say? He had considered walking out and letting her sleep, but that kindness would likely have had him on the receiving end of her silence, her back, and the sofa for the next few nights.

"You should eat something," he said as she took another swallow of coffee. Lucky strode in through the open sliding glass door, and Billy Jo walked over to it and slid it closed, then flicked the lock.

"I'll grab something later," she said, but Mark pulled open the fridge and retrieved an apple from the well-stocked fruit and vegetable drawer, real food instead of the prepackaged meals he'd once lived on.

"Here," he said and tossed it to her, and she turned and caught it one-handed. "Good catch. You ready?"

She made a face over the apple, then walked past him, sock footed, to the front door. "An apple, really? You feeling okay, Mark? This seems rather healthy," she said as she set it on the bench beside her, along with her coffee, and pulled on her brown ankle boots.

Mark watched his wife shrug on her blue fleece-lined coat as he pulled open the door. "Well, maybe we need to be a little more focused on what we're eating. You've been unusually tired, and you know the saying, an apple a day keeps the doctor away."

She lifted her hair, which was now past her shoulders, over the collar of her coat. Lucky was already out the door. Her gaze narrowed on Mark. "You were tossing and turning and kept me awake. That's why I'm tired."

"You mean I wasn't snoring?"

She reached for her coffee and purse on the bench, her unsmiling blue eyes not leaving his as she replied, "You were doing that, too."

Then she was out the door. Her apple was still on the bench, so he reached for it and let out a sharp whistle, calling out, "Your apple! Eat it," as he tossed it to her again.

He locked the door and walked over to his Jeep, where

his wife was taking a bite of the apple before pulling open the passenger door and letting Lucky into the back. Then she climbed in.

Mark was right behind her, sliding behind the wheel and starting the Jeep as he pulled his door closed. Billy Jo took another bite of the apple, then held it in her teeth as she pulled her seatbelt on. Mark reached for his sunglasses on the dash and slipped them on before putting the Jeep in gear and backing out.

"So does Walter know we're coming?" Billy Jo said.

Mark shook his head as he turned out onto the quiet main road. "Nope. Would give him time to prepare a story or just not be there. Showing up and catching him off guard will be priceless. It can tell me so much about someone, like whether he's hiding something."

She took another bite of the apple, and Lucky leaned over her seat and licked her ear. Billy Jo turned her head and kissed the dog. Mark made his way up onto the main road heading to the west side of the island.

"And what if he's, like, in bed, not up at the crack of dawn?" she said. She finished off her apple and dumped the core in the tiny trash bag attached to the glove box. He couldn't remember his vehicle ever having been so clean. That was part of married life and domestication, he figured—a part he liked, though he'd never admit as much.

"I'm a cop," he said. "It won't be the first time I've shown up on someone's doorstep and found them still in bed or doing other things." The kinds of things that made him have to clear his throat a couple times, involving compromising positions and a lack of clothes.

"You really enjoy this, don't you?"

He glanced over to Billy Jo, who was looking right at him, the go-mug to her lips. Her expression made him wonder what she was thinking at times. She was complicated, but damn, he loved her.

"You need to be a little more specific there, babe," he said.

She gave a hint of a smile as she pulled the mug away. "Rattling people, having the upper hand, as you say. Pretty much doing what you want, when you want, especially when you make people squirm because you're the law and they're mere peasants."

He took in the trees, the houses spread out. "Peasants? Seriously, I don't see people as mere peasants. What I often see are hooligans, troublemakers, people who don't give a shit about others, and people who believe they can buy and influence me or control what the average person says and does. I'm just done with that kind of shit. So yeah, if I come in hard, I'll apologize later. I think this is it." He took in an old wooden sign etched with the numbers 2436 and "Sage Farm." The driveway was narrow, with trees lining both sides, winding around and up a slight incline.

"Wow, nice house."

He didn't say anything in response as he took in the two-story timber frame that came into view. It had to be at least five thousand square feet, with a fenced-in garden and a big dog barking.

"Guess he has his own alarm," Billy Jo said. "He knows we're here."

The dog, a light lab, was running over to the Jeep as Mark pulled up in front of a three-car garage. He glanced once to Billy Jo and back to Lucky, who was whining, his face pressed to the side window.

"You stay here," he said, reaching back to run his hand over the dog, who whined again.

Billy Jo was already out of the Jeep, and as Mark

stepped out, a man appeared in the front door. He was tall, average build, wearing a brown work coat and blue jeans, a shotgun cradled in his arms.

"You lost?" he called out.

"Billy Jo, get back!" Mark yelled, his own gun already in his hand. "Put the gun down! I'm Chief Friessen." His heart thudded as he aimed the gun, not looking over to his wife but knowing she hadn't moved from beside the Jeep. "Put it down now! Won't ask a second time."

He waited one second and another, his heart thudding. The man bent down without pulling his gaze from Mark, then settled the shotgun on the ground, one hand up.

"You mind if I see your badge there, Chief? A man can't be too careful."

Mark kept his gun up in one hand and pulled back his jean jacket to show his badge fastened to the waistband of his blue jeans. "Billy Jo, you stay back," he called out again. He knew it had come out rather sharply, and he could feel the edge. He wished he hadn't been so quick to let her tag along.

The man was holding both hands up. His feet were shoved into a pair of heavy rain boots, and he wore a red checkered shirt under his open jacket. Judging by the dark whiskers on his face, he hadn't shaved.

"Can I put my hands down now, Chief?"

Mark headed for the shotgun and grabbed it. It was open, with two cartridges loaded. He holstered his own gun and emptied the shells onto the pavement. "You have any more weapons on you? Any inside?"

The man looked past him, evidently at Billy Jo, and then back to Mark. His brown eyes were more dark than light, and his hair had a messy natural wave, just touching his ears. "Just the shotgun here. I'm not carrying."

"Pull your jacket back, lift it, and turn around." Mark wasn't taking chances, not with his wife there. "You Walter Crandall?"

The man lifted his jacket up and turned around in a circle. "Yes, I'm Walter. Now how about answering a question for me? Why are you on my doorstep? Can I put my hands down now?"

Mark was still holding the shotgun. "Sure. Sorry, just not taking any chances. It makes me uncomfortable when someone has a loaded gun."

Walter said nothing for a second, looking past him again. "Can you tell me why you're on my property? And I'd like my gun back. Who is that with you?"

Mark reached down for the shells on the ground and shoved them in his pocket. "I'll just hold on to this for a bit, if you don't mind. That's my wife, Billy Jo, a social worker on the island. You have a moment to talk this morning?" It wasn't really a question, and maybe that was the reason for the rough laugh Walter let out before gesturing to the open door behind him.

"If I said no, Chief, somehow I don't think you'd leave. I suppose you can come in. You still haven't told me why you're here on my property."

Lucky was barking from the Jeep, but Mark didn't look back.

"Your dog friendly?" Walter said.

Mark shrugged. "Sure he is. Don't worry about him. He'll stay in the Jeep."

Walter had to be in his mid-forties, give or take. He said nothing, just staring at Mark with nothing friendly, jutting his chin. "Sarge, come here, boy," he called out and whistled to the lab, who started over to him. "You leaving your wife out here, too?" He looked around Mark. "Hey, there! Don't stand around. You can come on in."

The way Walter had talked around Mark to Billy Jo rubbed him the wrong way. He heard her footsteps and stepped back, still holding the shotgun, glancing over to her as she approached. He didn't have to say anything. He saw the questions in her blue eyes.

"I'm Walter, but I'm sure you know that already. Come on in. Was just making some breakfast for myself when I heard the ruckus outside." He kicked off his gumboots just inside the door and gestured as his dog trotted into the house. "Can I get either of you coffee?" he said, starting further inside.

Billy Jo angled her head and narrowed her eyes as she stared at the shotgun, and Mark pressed his hand to her back. "Well, that was an interesting way of meeting," she said, voice low.

"Didn't expect that greeting," was all Mark said in reply.

He stepped inside first, holding the shotgun. The open-concept living room had a showstopper view of the ocean, with a floor-to-ceiling window. He didn't know what he'd been looking for or expecting. The stone fireplace was massive, and the dog settled into a dog bed in front of it. In the kitchen, Walter was taking a pot off the stove.

Mark glanced back to Billy Jo. "Come on."

She looked down at his boots as she kicked off hers.

Mark only shook his head and gave his cowboy boots a wipe. "Not taking them off. Just stay close."

Her hand ran over his arm. "Always."

Damn, she was perfect.

He started over to the kitchen, where Walter was dumping steaming oatmeal from the pot into a bowl on the island. Everything was neat and tidy. A long table with two long benches, one on each side, was in front of another picture window.

"Nice place you have here. You live alone?" Mark said.

Walter put the pot in the sink and ran water into it before washing it out, rinsing it off, and flicking off the tap. He flicked his brown eyes over to Mark. "You have my shells. You want to put my shotgun down?" He was already drying the pot with a dishtowel, and he put it in the cupboard, then folded the dishtowel and hung it back up.

Mark walked over to the table and set the shotgun down.

Walter lifted the coffeepot, half full. "You didn't say if you wanted coffee."

"None for me." Billy Jo shoved her hands in the pockets of her coat.

"No, but thanks," Mark said, taking in the high ceiling, the open kitchen layout. A clock was ticking, he thought. "Anyone else here?"

"No one, just me and my dog. I just bought this place and moved here, but I have a feeling you know that already. Chief of police shows up at my place, who sent you? What is this really about? Because it's rather early for games, so let's skip them."

Walter pulled open a drawer, and Mark's hand was already on the butt of his gun. Walter lifted out a spoon slowly and put it beside the bowl. "Just a spoon, Chief. Easy there."

Mark just couldn't shake the off feeling he had. "No one sent me. Why would you think so?"

Walter let out a rough laugh. "Look, Chief, enough, please. I'm hungry and would rather you just come out and say whatever it is. Tell me who sent you. You here to warn me? Come on. We could dance around or you could just say it."

Mark knew he was frowning. "Warn you? Now, why would I do that? Look, not sure what you're talking about, but I was speaking with Shana yesterday, your ex, and she mentioned you showed up suddenly, wanting to make things right after walking out years ago…"

"Shana called you?" Walter cut in rather sharply, pressing both hands on the island, his shrewd gaze on Mark. He glanced over to Billy Jo. "Oh, and you're a social worker. She call you, too? Is this about my daughter, making sure I stay away from her?"

"Nothing official on my end," Billy Jo said. "Is there a reason Shana would call me? Because she hasn't."

She was right beside Mark, and he glanced down to her and then back to Walter. Something about this man still wasn't sitting right with him.

"So now you're fishing, sniffing around," Walter said, then gestured to Mark. "And you, what's your story for this surprise visit?"

"This is just about looking after my community and doing my due diligence. You're new to the island. I'm making sure there're no problems. Here to say hi, introduce myself, have a talk. Shana said you're a marketing executive for a big corporation."

Walter shoved a spoon in the steaming oatmeal and looked at them before walking over to the fridge and pulling it open to grab a carton of milk. He took a whiff, then poured some on the oatmeal. "I was the marketing director for the Wilson Foundation. If you want my exact title, it was deputy director. I was in charge of a multinational corporation, past tense. I'm retired now. Anything else you want to know? And what the hell is Shana doing, talking to you, anyway? You say she didn't call you? I'm having a hard time believing this is just a friendly call so you can get to know me." He put the milk back and closed the door. Mark noted how neat and tidy the kitchen was.

"Okay, you have me there," he said. "So how about

you tell me who you're expecting to show up here? You're expecting trouble?"

Walter reached for a small bowl with a lid and scooped some brown sugar from it onto the oatmeal. "Just call me a little paranoid, is all, with you, a stranger, showing up here unannounced. I don't know you or anyone on this island. Is there anything else I can help you with, Chief? Because I'm not some backwoods idiot who isn't aware of my rights, and it sounds to me as if you're questioning me. Are you questioning me, Chief? Causing me some trouble, violating my rights? How about we leave it at that? Is there anything else I can do for either of you?" The man shoved his spoon in the oatmeal and took a bite, dragging his gaze between Billy Jo and Mark.

"Just trying to figure out where you're coming from, Walter," Mark said. "You see, we have a nice peaceful island community here where folks are just living their lives, and they look to me to make sure this community stays safe and trouble free. You, I don't know you. In fact, I know nothing about you and why you've suddenly just shown up here."

"It's none of your business," Walter snapped. He dropped his spoon in his bowl with a clatter. "This is still a free country, and I can move anywhere I want to. I bought this place with my money, so the fact of the matter is that unless you show me a warrant, you are in fact trespassing. And how is it any of your business, Chief, if I want to make amends with my wife?"

"Ex-wife," Mark cut in, not missing the way his temper had spiked.

Walter gave his head a shake and stepped back. "You know, Chief, I think we're done here. Am I under arrest?"

"No, Walter, you're not under arrest. Just having a chat, is all."

The man nodded and then gestured toward the front door as he started walking. "Then I'm going to have to ask you to leave. We're done talking."

He was already at the front door. Billy Jo, who had been unusually quiet, nodded to signal that they needed to go. Mark walked behind her, his hand on her back, as he glanced back to the shotgun. Walter stood at the open front door, his hand on the edge of it, and Mark waited while Billy Jo shoved her feet into her ankle boots.

"Sorry for intruding, Walter," she said. "It was nice to meet you." She held out her hand, and Walter hesitated a second before taking it. "Mark, ready?" She said to him with determination in her blue eyes.

"Yeah," he said, stopping beside Walter. The man said nothing, but his gaze flickered with contempt and something else. He was Mark's height and build. He didn't look away, and Mark felt the open challenge.

"Mark, are you coming?" Billy Jo called out quite sharply.

Mark kept walking, following his wife to the Jeep.

"Oh, and, Chief, one more thing," Walter called out.

Mark stopped and turned.

"If you want to talk to me again, you can do it through my lawyer," he said. Then he went inside and closed the door.

Mark kept walking and climbed into his Jeep, where he started the engine, his hand on the gear shift, as he listened to Billy Jo fasten her seatbelt.

"Well, what do you make of that?" she said.

Mark ran his hand over his face and let out a sigh, taking in the big beautiful house, the size of the property. He couldn't put his finger on what was bothering him. "He's hiding something."

"You think?" The sarcasm dripped. Mark looked over

to the one person who always had his back. "So now what?"

"I do what I do best," he said as he pulled back up the drive. "Find out exactly what his secrets are."

Eight

"You can take my car if you need to," Lacy said to Billy Jo as she lingered inside the station. Mark was now behind closed doors in his office with Carmen, all because Gail had decided to show up and Mark hadn't told either of his colleagues to expect her. Gail was standing awkwardly by the window, her dark rain jacket still on. The tension in the stationhouse was anything but welcoming.

"No, that's fine," Billy Jo said. "I already sent Pam a text and let her know I'm not coming in this morning." She took another look over to Gail, knowing that this was all on her. Damn, she really did look two seconds from being out the door. Just then, Billy Jo's cell phone rang, and she pulled it out to see Pam's name on the screen. "Shit," was all she said. She hesitated only a second before answering. "Hey, Pam, did you get my message?"

"That's why I'm calling. Lisa was just asking when you're coming in. You're supposed to be reviewing case files with her first thing this morning, and now she's up in arms because she's waiting and you're not here."

Billy Jo turned and pressed a hand over her face. She loved her job but hated Lisa. Right, she wasn't supposed to hate people. "Give me strength," she said under her breath.

"What was that?"

"Nothing. Never mind. Just thinking out loud. Put her on the phone, but, Pam, I've got something to take care of, so I won't be in this morning. I'm only a phone call away if something comes up, though. And I mean that. Call me. Don't just give anything to Lisa to handle."

"Yes, yes, I know, okay? Here she is," Pam said. Billy Jo heard Lisa in the background. There was a rustle of papers.

"Did you forget we had a meeting this morning to go over my caseload?" Lisa said. Her voice was always laced with challenge.

"Something came up, is all. It happens. I did not forget." Actually, she had, and she fought the urge to snarl at being called out. She was so glad she had her back to everyone.

"So what am I supposed to do now, sit here and stare into space? You know I don't appreciate having to get your approval before I do my job. I trained for this, and I do understand and know my job. In fact, believe it or not, I actually went to school just like you."

"Not this again. Do you need a refresher on how you overstepped and nearly destroyed one family? Remember Nathan and Grace and their girls? That wasn't an oopsie and now everything's okay. Emotional scars sometimes never go away." Billy Jo gave it right back to her, knowing that Lisa wouldn't hear a word she said. She was so damn opinionated and difficult, refusing to ever concede when she was wrong. Billy Jo sometimes wondered what she'd done to deserve this challenging person in her life.

"I made a judgement call, which is what we do. I'm sure you've done the same. Our job is about the kids first, and if we suspect anything, we yank them."

Billy Jo let the phone slide away from her mouth as she stared up to the ceiling, knowing she was ramming her head against the wall, as this girl would not listen. "Which is why you go over everything with me first, because you still don't know the people here. There are always underlying circumstances, a different story. And, for the record, Lisa, I've said this before. I have never yanked kids unless there is no other option. Unless there is something urgent, you can spend the morning pulling all the files for all the approved families and taking a closer look at them."

"Excuse me, Billy Jo," Lisa cut in quite sharply, "but the state has approved them already, and you know the people here remember. So why would I waste my time there? And what about the missing kids?"

Billy Jo heard the door to Mark's office open, and she glanced behind her to him and Carmen, giving him a nod. Damn, did she love him. "Which kids are missing?" She turned away again, wondering if she'd missed an email.

"Runaways, I guess. Two from the same home."

"From where, here?"

Papers rustled. "Teemonts, over in Port Angeles."

Billy Jo pressed her hand to her forehead and made herself pull in a breath. "I'm confused. Port Angeles? That's not our jurisdiction. Was our office notified?"

"While I've been sitting, waiting for you, I was in the database for the state and came across the flag and notice of the missing kids."

Billy Jo had no idea how to talk to Lisa at times, let alone understand where she was coming from. She could honestly say she'd left her speechless. "Is this recent? From what part of the database? Where are you finding this?"

And how come she didn't know about it, she wondered? She turned and looked over to Mark again. It was becoming automatic, the way he seemed to know she was watching him, needed him, or that something was wrong.

"When you go into the state database, you can filter through the counties and the files," Lisa said. "Sometimes there's a flag, but sometimes there's nothing, just a file among thousands and thousands in no particular order. But I just go through them when I have time, looking at ones in the surrounding areas, looking for patterns…"

"Wait, stop." She lifted a hand. Mark was walking her way, and Carmen and Lacy were talking with Gail. For a moment, Billy Jo felt as if the rug had been yanked from under her. "So no alert was sent out?"

"No, I was just searching."

"You do this a lot, search through the database?"

There was silence for a second. Mark was now standing right in front of her, gesturing at the phone.

"It's not a crime, you know," Lisa said, defensiveness back in her snarky voice.

"That's not what I meant, Lisa. What I'm saying is I don't remember seeing these files, the flags you say are on there."

"Well, you won't see it unless you look for it. It's not on the first page or in the menu. You find it by clicking back-links and then more links."

She angled her head, really listening. "So how did you stumble across this?"

Again, there was silence on the other end.

"Lisa, seriously, I want to know," Billy Jo said, "because it sounds to me as if it's been hidden."

"Hidden in plain sight, I guess. There is no main link. You have to go to a page and then another page, click some links, and there it is. I guess it's something I've always been good at, digging around, finding things online that no one else does—you know, the proverbial rabbit hole everyone ignores or can't be bothered with?"

Mark glanced over his shoulder and back to her. She sensed his impatience.

"You know what?" Billy Jo said. "Keep looking. Keep doing what you're doing, Lisa, and when I get there, I want you to show me where you found this online."

Silence again. Billy Jo's heartbeat picked up just like it did every time something went wrong.

"Okay," Lisa said. "Anything specific you want me to look for?"

Billy Jo nodded to herself. "Start with the kids who are missing…or anything unusual."

"Sure, yeah, I can do that. But you're not coming in?"

"I'll be in later, an hour," Billy Jo said, then hung up and let out a heavy sigh.

"What was that about?" Mark said.

"Lisa was poking around in some files I didn't know existed and came across two missing kids."

Mark didn't pull his gaze. "Two kids are missing from here? Lacy, is there a report of missing kids?" he called out, turning away before she could finish.

"Not from here, Mark. Port Angeles." Billy Jo touched his arm, and he dragged his distracted gaze back to her. "Lisa found a bunch of files in our database after digging around. I don't know where they were, but it sounds like you have to really look. Anyway, I don't know anything else, but she's going to dig around some more for me and show me when I get back in."

Mark nodded and let his gaze linger. "You let me know if you want me to do some digging, too."

"Always. So, everything good here?" She didn't know

what to make of Carmen, who was now sitting behind her desk, the phone to her ear, or Lacy, who had said something to Gail and then walked away to the back. Gail was still standing by the window.

"Carmen wants to know if I've lost my mind. Her exact words," Mark said, his voice low. Billy Jo could see how uncomfortable Gail was from the way she was now watching them. He let out a heavy sigh. "You got to go deal with Lisa? If you give me a minute, I'll drive you home so you can get your car." Boy, he really was distracted.

"And what about Gail?"

Mark glanced over his shoulder again and then back to her, and she knew he understood. He shrugged, and she followed him as he strode over to window, where Gail was likely doing her best to stay out of the way.

"Sorry about all this, Gail," he said. "I didn't have a chance to fill Carmen in."

"Yeah, the minute I walked through that front door, I knew it was a bad idea. I should have turned around and walked back out."

Billy Jo took in Carmen, who was still on the phone. She wondered if she could hear, or maybe not. She was scribbling something, and her brow furrowed. Billy Jo didn't know exactly where Carmen stood in the tarring and feathering of Gail.

"Mark, you fill Gail in on our visit with Walter Crandall this morning?" Billy Jo said.

Just then, she heard yelling, a commotion outside, and she shot a look to the window to see Merv, the dining room manager from across the road, practically dragging an old woman toward the station.

"Shit," Mark said under his breath.

Billy Jo just stared. The older woman was swatting at

Merv. Mark was already out the door, and Carmen was off the phone, on her feet now, right behind him out the door, which was wide open.

"Well, well, well, looks like old Merv has had enough of Tulsi Lee's shenanigans," Gail said with an odd smile. She glanced over to Billy Jo and shrugged. "Tulsi and her husband, Charlie, are known for dining and dashing and taking anything and everything that's not nailed down. She's smart as a whip, that one. Approaching eighty, and she plays it up good. Still carries that big, bulky bag, I see. Wonder what's stuffed in there? She can talk her way out of anything, using her age and the helpless old lady act."

"How do you know?" Billy Jo dragged her gaze from the commotion outside back to Gail.

"It's what she does. Most don't even see it. Been doing this a long time. To set Merv off like that, guarantee she tried to pull something on him. She'll play the age card if she can't lie her way out of it, say she forgot to pay. Been doing it for years. Guess Merv finally caught on. I bet if someone looks in her bag, they'll find salt and pepper shakers, some tableware too. You know how much goes missing in stores? I would hazard a guess that she pays for one thing and stuffs five others in that big bag of hers. And those are only the tricks I know of. Guarantee she does way more that I don't know."

Billy Jo dragged her gaze back to the window and the commotion outside. "And she gets away with it? Are you sure? She doesn't look the type."

"Really? Explain to me what the type looks like." Gail had pinned her to the spot, narrowing her gaze.

"You're right," Billy Jo said. "My bad. Came out wrong. But, seriously, she looks like the grandma next door."

"And she plays that well. You know what I learned

about Tulsi and Charlie? They have a pretty penny, those two, even though they come off cheap as anything. Seriously, they really do nickel and dime people to death."

Billy Jo frowned, taking in the old woman and Merv, who was furious. Mark was having Merv take a step back, his arms crossed, and Carmen had slid her arm over the old woman's shoulders.

"You sure this time? I mean, look at her. She appears shaken, distraught."

Gail tsked under her breath. "It's called acting, Billy Jo. A damn good performance she can pull off, and most people can't see past it. Let's just hope Mark doesn't fall for the helpless little old lady con job."

Billy Jo took in Gail again and glanced back to the window. The old lady was being sent on her way nicely by Carmen, and Billy Jo noted the smile on her face. Merv was suddenly on the wrong side of Mark. Gail gave a heavy sigh.

"She played him," Billy Jo said. For a moment, she thought Mark was going to pull out his cuffs.

"She did indeed," Gail said.

"Still think you're not needed here?"

Gail appeared uneasy, stiffening and stepping away from the window.

The door opened, and Mark dragged in Merv and gestured sharply, barking, "Park your ass in that chair."

Billy Jo raised her brows as Gail gave her an odd look, her arms cross tightly over her chest. "Now or never, Gail. Come on," she said.

Another heavy sigh. "You just don't let up, do you?"

What could she say? She still had her own demons that haunted her. "Can't. Wouldn't have a peaceful night's sleep then, you know."

"Yeah, I do," Gail said, then took a step around Billy Jo and touched her shoulder as she said, "Mark, can I have a minute?"

Mark stopped mid-step to his office. His gaze went to Billy Jo first, then Gail, confusion in his amazing blue eyes. "Let me handle this first," he said.

"Yeah, about that," Gail said. "Let me guess. Merv alleges that Tulsi and her husband ordered lunch and drinks and then left without paying, and she played the forgetful old lady card or, my favorite, says she left cash on the table and someone must have taken it? And you're probably missing table settings, too, right, Merv?"

"The table behind Tulsi left cash," Merv said. "My waitress Leanne saw it, but when she went to get it, it was gone. I just tried telling the chief, but he wants to read me the riot act about putting my hands on an old lady, saying I could be charged with assault."

Mark was glancing between Gail and Merv, pulling his hand over his face in confusion. He gestured to Gail. "My office?"

She only nodded and strode in ahead of him, and he followed and closed the door. That left a quiet Lacy behind her desk, going through files, and Merv, who didn't look too happy.

"Didn't know Gail was working back here again," he said. "Not sure that's a great idea."

Lacy flicked her gaze to Billy Jo. Merv was still sitting in a chair at Mark's old desk, wearing a black t-shirt and blue jeans, his hair a mix of dark and grey.

"Really?" Billy Jo said. "If I were you, I'd be grateful." She couldn't help herself.

The face Merv made was priceless. "How so?"

"Right now, she's in there, saving your ass," Lacy said,

gesturing at Mark's office, before Billy Jo could say anything.

Merv just stared at her, then dragged his gaze over to the closed office door. Billy Jo saw his moment of understanding, but instead of appearing grateful, he seemed to settle in his chair and said nothing.

Billy Jo climbed out of Lacy's older Tracker and closed the door, taking in the DCFS field office, with its tinted windows and locked glass door. She shoved her key in the lock and stepped inside, then flicked the lock behind her.

"Hey, I thought you weren't coming in this morning?" Pam appeared from around the corner, wearing a brown sweater over a white blouse and dark pants. The office was quiet and cool, and the lights were dimmed. With the squeak of a chair, Lisa slid back from around the sectioned-off area, saying nothing but tracking Billy Jo's every step as she stuffed Lacy's keys in her purse.

"Mark is in the middle of something, so I borrowed Lacy's car," she said. "I wanted to have a look at what you found, Lisa."

At least Mark was listening to Gail now, and Gail hadn't appeared to be one step out the door before Billy Jo left, but she wasn't about to share any of that with Pam. Then there was Lisa, who never smiled, sitting in that wheeled office chair in a tan tank top with a black lace cover, nothing Billy Jo would ever wear, and a jean skirt hiked up over bare legs, her feet shoved in flat ankle boots. Her brown hair was in a ponytail, and she wore dark rimmed glasses that only accentuated the pissed-off expression she always had for Billy Jo. She really did have an odd sense of fashion. Billy Jo didn't miss the wariness in her eyes now.

"You're not cold?" She just couldn't help herself.

"Of course not." Lisa pulled her arms over her chest, and Billy Jo could sense she was ready to butt heads with her, so she made herself look away. Pam was shaking her head, having had to run interference between them a few times already.

"So tell me about these kids and what you found," Billy Jo said, flicking her gaze back to Lisa, who stared at her a second before using her heels to drag her chair back to her desk, where a laptop was open.

She tapped the keyboard and mousepad, and the screen lit up. "As I said to you already over the phone, I thought they were from a group home up in Teemonts, Port Angeles, but they were actually from a family up there. Here're the notes, pretty vague. A boy and girl, eight and twelve, not related, labeled as runaways here. I went ahead and sent an inquiry to the social worker about them." She glanced back to Billy Jo as if expecting to be shut down.

"Well, don't keep me in suspense," Billy Jo said. "What did the social worker say?"

Lisa dragged her gaze back to the laptop. "Nothing, didn't respond."

"Give it a few days. I'm sure they'll get back to you."

"I emailed a week ago, then sent a follow-up three days ago and left a message this morning."

And she was only telling her this now? Something

about the way Lisa spoke always came off as arrogant, but Billy Jo had to remind herself this was about two missing kids, not her ego.

"I see. What about a police report?"

Lisa shook her head. "There's a file number with the local police, but again they're marked as runaways. Since you haven't yelled at me yet, I may as well go for broke here: I pulled up all the files of kids in this state and then the rest of the country—which, by the way, took me a little more work, as it wasn't all in one place. It was as if someone with zero computer skill put it together, or maybe that was deliberate." Lisa looked up to her and sighed, maybe at the way Billy Jo wasn't smiling. "There are more than fifty thousand kids marked as runaways now and more than sixty-five thousand marked as missing. Let that sink in. That's over one hundred thousand children who should be in a home where someone's watching out for them, but not only are they missing and unaccounted for, it appears no one is looking for them. Just on a hunch, I started doing some cross-referencing and looking for patterns, and when doing that I found a case in Yakima of a man charged with production and possession of child pornography. He took a plea, no jail time, but I had a weird feeling and thought, why not take a deep dive down the rabbit hole? Since I have all this spare time on my hands…"

A sick knot pulled in Billy Jo's stomach. She hoped Lisa wasn't going to say what she thought she would. Maybe that was obvious from the look on her face, because smugness was staring up at her now. "And…" She gestured towards the laptop. "Come on, Lisa, no games. Just say it. What did you find? Seriously, that many kids are just gone?"

Lisa pulled off her glasses and rubbed them with her

shirt before shoving them back on and clicking the keyboard, pulling up a small news article from a small-town paper. "Yup. He's a foster parent, and wouldn't you know, he's still approved. Still has kids. What do you want to guess he's still putting out child pornography? Kind of leaves you with a warm and fuzzy feeling, doesn't it? It sure seems like he's got an ample pool of kids to pick from."

Billy Jo realized Lisa was serious. She leaned in. "How many kids does he have?" And who could she call, she thought? Because someone was going to get fired over this.

"He's had kids in and out of his place with his wife for twelve years," Lisa said. "Roughly thirty-five in total. Funny thing, I can't find a record of what happened to roughly ten of them. Oh, and you may love this. Apparently, two of the kids volunteered to be part of some drug trial, though I don't know how a three-year-old and seven-year-old can consent to anything. The three-year-old has since died. Not sure what happened to the other one, as there's nothing else in the file. I didn't get a chance to poke around and see how much money the pharmaceutical company paid out to this guy for the use of the kids as guinea pigs. All of these files go off in all kinds of directions. Even I was starting to go cross-eyed. I started creating a spreadsheet of the kids, the families, the social workers, the counties…"

Billy Jo angled her head. Lisa suddenly sounded so far away, and the ringing in her ears had come out of nowhere. She blinked, fighting a wave of dizziness, and then suddenly everything went black.

SHE WAS ON THE FLOOR, staring up at the ceiling. How the hell had she gotten on the floor? Her vague awareness slowly returned, and a hand was shaking her.

"Billy Jo, wake up. Answer me…"

It was Pam, she thought. She blinked again, and maybe that was her who groaned. The ringing in her ears was starting to fade, and all she was aware of was her breath, voices, and pounding on the door. She stared at the commercial drop ceiling and a stain she hadn't known was there.

Pam was leaning over her, and the panic in her expression and her raised penciled-in brows was priceless. "Are you okay? Damn, girl, you just keeled right over…"

Someone was pounding on the door again.

"Lisa, go and get that," Pam said.

"I'm fine," Billy Jo said. "Shit, what happened?" She lifted her hand to her forehead and started to sit up, vaguely hearing the door and Mark's voice.

"Where is she? What the hell happened?" Mark was right there, and Lisa was behind him.

Billy Jo was now sitting up and blinking. Nothing like this had ever happened before. Mark was on the ground beside her, his hand on her back, helping her up.

"I have no idea," she said. "I must be hungry. I blacked out for a second."

"You keeled right over. You hit the floor hard," Pam said. She had pulled a chair over for her, and Mark held her by the arm as she sat.

"Pam, can you get Billy Jo some water," he said. When she returned, he took the glass from her and held it to Billy Jo. "Drink this."

She flicked her gaze up to him. "Stop looking so worried. Wait, why are you here?"

"I called Mark as soon as you fainted," Pam said,

standing on the other side of him in front of her, arms crossed.

"I was out that long?" Why couldn't she remember anything?

"I was a block away already when Pam called," he said. "I think you need to see a doctor."

"I'm not seeing a doctor, Mark. I'm fine. Told you, I'm just hungry. Other than that apple, I haven't eaten anything. And I didn't faint. I don't faint…"

Billy Jo thought Mark cursed under his breath. She took another swallow of water and held the glass out to Pam. "Okay, Lisa, before I passed out, you said you were doing a spreadsheet."

Mark rested his hands on his hips after dragging one over his face hearing a scrape of whiskers.

Lisa looked to Mark as if Billy Jo had gone off script. "Yes, as I said, I started creating a spreadsheet of all the missing kids, their ages, ethnicities, where they were, and making notes of any investigations."

Mark frowned and was now looking at Lisa. "What are you talking about? What missing kids?" He dragged his gaze back to Billy Jo. Her very protective husband had gone into cop mode.

"Lisa has been housecleaning, going through the family services database and all the missing kids. Isn't that right, Lisa?"

Lisa blinked.

Mark frowned, looking between her and Billy Jo. "Is this what you were talking about earlier, the missing kids?"

Billy Jo nodded. "Not just missing. No one is looking for them."

Mark let out a heavy sigh. "I think you'd better start at the beginning and tell me everything."

Lisa suddenly had a spooked look. "I'm not going to get in trouble, am I?"

Exactly what Billy Jo hadn't expected. "No, Lisa, you're not," she said. "Just show Mark what you found, and then I want you to keep looking."

She had realized that Lisa, evidently, was really good at something she wasn't.

CHAPTER

Ten

"You know, Mark, I'm fine to drive," Billy Jo said from the passenger side as he climbed behind the wheel of his Jeep and waved to Lacy, who was driving away in her Tracker after Pam had gone and picked her up.

"The hell you are," he said. "You passed out. You were on the floor when I walked in, and yeah, I may have been just around the corner, but one look at you and how pale you were, how shaky…I want you to see a doctor. You've been really tired lately, no matter what you say. Something's wrong."

Lucky gave Billy Jo's face a lick, and she reached back and rubbed him. Mark started the Jeep.

"So how did it go with Gail and Merv?" she said, changing the subject, he knew, so she didn't have to talk about herself.

"I still can't get past the fact that Tulsi isn't a helpless old lady but a career criminal who skated under the radar," he said. "She played me. What I can't figure out is why she was trembling. So damn convincing. Merv said she paid, but with money left by customers at another table. He'd figured out what she was doing and planted it, and she took the bait. Carmen is on her way over to have a chat with her. Like, how does someone pull that off, especially someone her age? Gail did her homework on Tulsi a while back. Tomorrow I plan to talk to her about everyone else on the island." He was beyond pissed, because the gut feelings he got about people had completely failed him with Tulsi. "Gail knows the island and the people here in ways I don't. You want me to say you were right?"

There it was, the hint of a smile as he shoved the Jeep in gear and backed out. "Could you say that again? I'm not sure I heard you."

He pulled out of the parking lot and glanced over to his wife. She didn't smile very often, but damn, when she did… "Don't be a smartass," he said. "So, since Merv is unlikely to give us a table at his restaurant, what do you say we stop at the Dog and Whistle, grab an early dinner, a couple burgers? Or we could drive over to the hospital and have a doctor take a look at you. The latter I would prefer."

"A burger sounds great. So does that mean you had a chance to talk with Gail about our visit with Walter this morning?" There she went, taking the subject of her off the table as always.

"Burger it is," he said, "but I'm not letting it drop about your health, Billy Jo. If the shoe were on the other foot, you wouldn't let it slide. Just saying."

She looked straight ahead, no give in her expression. He let out a heavy sigh, knowing he was pushing too hard. She frustrated him sometimes with how unyielding she could be.

"Gail also suggested a visit to Shana," he said. "She isn't surprised Walter isn't willing to talk to me. She did say he'll likely do his homework on me before I drop in again. Of course, I said, what the hell is that supposed to mean? Why does he think I'm going to drop in again? Gail just smiled and said, 'Come on, Mark. You and I both know you are. You're just waiting for the right moment to show up again. He knows you're digging around in his life, his past, so he's doing the very same thing to you.'"

Gail had tossed him another warning to be careful, too, though he'd keep that part to himself.

Billy Jo was quiet for a moment. "Mark, you know how Lisa is digging around in the database for all those kids labeled runaways or missing? I just don't understand why there isn't a bigger, better search being done. That's a lot of kids. Are you really going to take the spreadsheet Lisa has put together and look into it? I know you feel it's important to look into everyone on the island, and I understand why, but these are kids no one gives a shit about. I get a kid running away, but just going missing? I've seen it before, but the number she gave me was jaw-dropping.

"What I really want to know is where these kids are going, because a kid on the street would stick out. These kids have no voice, and I'm really starting to get the impression that I'm not making any difference at all. Seriously, if those were my files, kids in my charge, there would be an all-out manhunt for each of them. I wouldn't let the police conveniently mark them as runaways. I would not leave any stone unturned. That many kids, and no one is looking for them?

"Mark, I can't shake the idea that throughout the entire system I work for, the system I was once in, which is the reason I do what I do, no one gives a shit about these kids." She stopped talking mid-rant and let out a heavy sigh. "I was just hoping I could change something. The more I see, and after everything you and I have had thrown our way, it seems like this entire system is a front for something, as if it's being deliberately mismanaged. I know it sounds ridiculous, and government mismanagement goes on everywhere, but it can't happen here. These are kids. There has to be more accountability. There have to be stronger controls, and whoever was responsible for allowing those two children to take part in medical experiments should be in jail."

Mark pulled into the parking lot of the Dog and Whistle, which was half full in the early afternoon. His wife was upset. He could hear it in her voice. He turned off the Jeep and reached back to rub Lucky, saying, "You stay here." Then he opened his door and looked over to Billy Jo. She was distracted, venting, and likely going to lose sleep. "Told you before, Billy Jo: kids and animals. I will leave no stone unturned, and that includes looking into everything Lisa finds. You're right, there has been a shitshow here, and I promise you I will look. You know I will, even though stepping on toes in another sheriff's jurisdiction will not go over well."

Billy Jo nodded, making a face as she looked out the window and then back to him. "But you'll do it anyway for the kids."

Mark climbed out, keeping his window rolled down. "For the kids, always. Stay, Lucky," he said, then waited for Billy Jo as she walked around the vehicle.

She slid her hand around his arm, leaning into him for a second as they walked. "You know I love you, right?"

He pressed a kiss to the top of her head. Billy Jo was not known for saying she loved him, because that vulnerability was her no-go zone.

"Damn straight I do," he said. "But listen up. I still want you to get a checkup for me, okay? You scared me." He hesitated at the door.

She wouldn't look at him at first, but then she did, making another face. "If I don't feel better, then I will, but I told you I'm just hungry. I've been skipping meals, is all."

He pulled open the door, knowing that was as good as he was going to get, and was hit by the sound of the country jukebox playing in the dim room. He slid his hand over Billy Jo's back, letting it linger as he looked around. People were at the bar, a few of the tables taken.

"Busy for this time of day," he said. "There's a table over there." He gestured, and Billy Jo started walking over to a small round table close to the bar. She pulled out a wooden chair with a scrape, and he spotted Shana coming their way as he sat across from her.

"Chief, what can I get you?" Shana gave the empty table a wipe with a cloth.

"Kitchen open? Hoping for a couple burgers," he said.

"Yeah, the cook just got here," Shana said. "He'll need a few minutes to warm the grill."

"Great." Mark gestured across the table. "Shana, this is my wife, Billy Jo. She's a social worker here on the island."

"I think we've met before." Shana looked right at Billy Jo, who nodded.

"Yes. Seen you with your little girl, Haley. She looks just like you."

There it was, pleasantries over.

"So, fries with your burgers?" Shana said.

"Works for me, and coffee, too, if you have some on. Billy Jo…?"

Shana nodded. "Coffee. I'll make a fresh pot," she said.

Billy Jo leaned back in her chair. "I'll steal some of Mark's fries," she said, "but can you add a salad for me instead? And just a water with a couple of lemon wedges."

"You got it," Shana said, then was walking away.

Mark glanced at the bar. A man sitting there was

watching Shana, and it took Mark a second to realize who it was. "Well, look at that, at the bar." He nodded to Walter, who was looking right at him, leaning on the bar with his forearms. Walter nodded back.

"What is he doing here?" Billy Jo leaned forward and glanced over her shoulder again. "I thought Shana didn't want anything to do with him."

Walter said something to Shana, who only shook her head before walking their way. "Here's your water," she said, setting down the glass in front of Billy Jo. "Coffee will be a few minutes, Chief."

"Thanks, Shana. I see Walter is here." Mark jutted his chin in his direction. Walter hadn't looked away, even while taking a swallow from a pint of beer.

Shana glanced over her shoulder, her hands on her hips. "Yeah. Showed up here not long before you. Had a bee in his bonnet because you paid him a visit. Seemed to think I put you up to it. But I was clear with him. I already told him I don't need anyone to speak for me, and I sure as shit am not sending the cops to his doorstep. You tell him I sent you?"

Mark shook his head, leaning back. Shana's eyes held an edge. She was pissed off, maybe. "Nope, I didn't. But I was greeted with a shotgun, which has me wondering who he's expecting. Didn't like me in his business."

She shook her head and lifted her hands. "Doesn't much like anyone in his business. You take anything in your coffee, Chief?" She was done talking about Walter.

"Just black, thanks, Shana."

As she walked away again, Walter tracked her every move. He asked Shana something, but she just waved him off and gestured to his beer, then poured Mark's coffee. Mark didn't know what that was about, but she didn't look as if she had time for him. Billy Jo said nothing, dragging her gaze back to Mark.

"What do you make of that?" she said. Walter had slid off the high stool.

"Not sure, but I guess I'm going to find out."

Walter Crandall, holding his beer, was walking their way. "Chief, you following me now?"

Something about the man had that unsettled feeling stirring in Mark's gut again.

"Nope, just here for a late lunch, is all. You remember my wife, Billy Jo."

Billy Jo only lifted her glass and took a swallow of water.

"Walter, you behaving yourself?" Shana said, walking around him to set a mug of coffee on the table in front of Mark. "Your coffee, Chief." She dumped a couple creamers and sugar packets on the table with a napkin.

Walter shook his head, made a face. "I want a word with you, Shana."

Shana glanced to Mark. "Your burgers are just going on. Shouldn't be too long." She turned to Walter and lifted her hand. "I'm busy. Finish your beer and then be on your way. It's on the house," she said, then walked away.

"Pretty sure she isn't interested in talking to you," Mark said, unable to help himself. He reached for a creamer, likely because of how late in the day it was, and dumped it in his coffee. "So what are you doing here?" He gave his mug a swirl, leaned back in his chair, and looked up at Walter.

Walter rested his pint on the table and set both hands on the back of the empty chair, looking first to Billy Jo and then over to Mark. "You know, Chief, I do not need to explain to you what I'm doing here, having a beer, talking with my wife. It's really not your concern. A word of advice? Remember how it felt to be a young deputy without backup because you were convinced ratting out your fellow cops was the right thing to do."

Mark froze with his mug to his lips. He reminded himself of what Gail had said and made himself take a sip before putting the coffee down. Billy Jo was watching him, but he couldn't look away from Walter. "You been looking into me?"

Walter dragged his gaze over to Billy Jo. "You should have a word with your husband," he said. "Sometimes, those nests you start poking around in have snakes hiding in them, poisonous ones. You two have a nice life here. Don't you be worrying about me. If I were you, Chief and Mrs. Friessen, you two should just stick to being newly-weds, landscaping that new property you bought, looking after your dog and that three-legged cat, and keeping nuisance locals from stirring up trouble. I would really hate to see problems tear apart your happily ever after."

"That sounds like a threat," Mark said. "Are you threatening us, Walter?" He pushed back his chair and stood up. He was the same height as Walter, but the man didn't cower in the least, and he didn't look away.

"No, that was just a friendly warning, Chief. You two enjoy your lunch," Walter said, then took one step back and another before looking over to Shana, who was standing behind the bar, watching them. "Shana, we'll talk later," he said as he started walking, looking right and left at the people in the bar. Then he opened the door and walked out.

"Mark, what the hell was that about?" Billy Jo said. "How did he know about my cat, our house…?"

He flicked his gaze to Billy Jo, seeing the spooked look as she dragged her gaze from the door to him. Mark sat back in his chair, very aware of the table behind him. That unsettled feeling was back. "Doing his homework on me, but damn, he's hitting too close to home."

"Here're your burgers." Shana put their plates down in front of them. "You mind telling me what that was about?" She flicked her gaze to the door and reached for the half-full glass of beer still on the table.

"Your ex apparently doesn't like anyone looking into him," Mark said. "Seems he's done his homework on me and my wife. If you have a minute, Shana, I'd really like for you to tell me what it is he's hiding, why he's really here. A man who digs into a cop's life and family, just how dangerous is he?"

Shana said nothing. She appeared to hesitate before letting out a sigh. "I don't know why he's here, really. Is he dangerous?" She lifted her hands and shook her head. "He's secretive, smart, but he's never laid a hand on me. You evidently stepped on his toes, his ego, or into his business. Chief, you stirred things up with him, and now he walks into my bar, into my life, and his crap becomes mine. I already told you I'm done with him. What do you want with him, anyway? Has he done something?"

Mark glanced at Billy Jo, who was watching Shana. "Just doing my due diligence as chief, making sure anyone who shows on the island isn't bringing a problem."

Shana nodded and shrugged. "Fair enough. Just do me a favor. You and Walter hash it out somewhere else, and don't bring this into my bar. I'll get you two some utensils and ketchup. Can I get you anything else?"

"Some salt. Thanks, Shana," Billy Jo cut in. She reached over for a fry as Shana walked away. "She's right, you know."

"How so?" Mark dragged his gaze to the door again.

"He's not her problem. She wants nothing to do with him. But please look into him. Find out everything about him and why he's really moved back to the island." She took a bite of the fry.

"Already on it," he said.

Maybe, after they finished eating, they should stop at home. Mark would take another look at their place, test the locks on the doors and the windows, and check on the damn cat.

Mark was hovering. Billy Jo could feel him watching her closely every time he thought she wasn't looking. She listened to him in his office on the phone. Gail was sitting at Carmen's desk, likely because it was as far away from the front door as possible, and Lacy was on the phone, as well.

Billy Jo had filled Lucky's dish with fresh water. As she turned around, feeling out of sorts, the burger sitting heavy in her stomach, she took in the stack of files Gail was sorting through, notes pinned to the front of each. The late afternoon sun was dipping, and Billy Jo knew Mark tracked her every move as she started across the station.

Gail didn't look up at her as she said, "He's worried, is all. You scared him."

How did Gail do that?

Billy Jo sat in the chair reserved for criminals by the side of the desk and leaned back. "I was hungry. Now I'm not. He's making too much of it. You know he drove home right after we left Shana's bar and told me to stay put in the Jeep while he went to check on my cat? Then I watched him walk around the house, checking all the windows. I knew what he was doing. He climbed back in the Jeep, and the only thing he said was that he was going to look into getting an alarm and better locks on the windows."

Gail gave a hint of a smile, then flicked her gaze to the door as it opened. Carmen had walked in, and from the way she looked over to Gail, Billy Jo could feel the tension.

"Sorry, Carmen, give me a minute," Gail said. "I'll move to the back." Damn, she sounded so rattled.

Carmen lifted her hand. "No, it's fine," she said, then kept walking. Billy Jo had to crane her neck to see Carmen at her desk. For a moment, no one said anything, and all she could hear was Mark on the phone. Then Carmen flicked her gaze to Billy Jo, the files on the desk, and Gail behind it.

"So how did it go with Tulsi and Charlie?" Gail said as she closed up a file and reached for another. She held it out to Carmen, who frowned and took it.

"You have any idea how it feels to be scammed by who I thought was a sweet old lady?" Carmen said. "I was so pissed that I fired up the sirens and blew past a few cars on the way to their place. I blasted the siren several times as I pulled into their driveway so their neighbors knew I was coming in hot and heavy. But you know who I was greeted by? Their son, who just so happens to be a lawyer. The only thing he wanted to talk about was the apparent bruising on Tulsi's arm, which she's saying was put there by Merv. So what is this?" Carmen opened the file and frowned.

Billy Jo heard Lacy scoot out her squeaky chair and walk into the back.

"File and notes on Tulsi and her husband," Gail said. "As for the assault, their slithering snake of a son will attempt to harass Mark into pressing charges on Merv, or he'll just go over his head to the council and mayor. He'll also serve the restaurant with a slew of lawsuits, allegations that are ridiculous and frivolous but will tie Merv up in court for years, with lawyer fees that will bankrupt him and his family. Tulsi and her husband are takers, and they raised their son in their image. Sure, they appear to be a respectable older couple you'd always give a pass to, and they've used that to their advantage. They've taken from people their entire lives. I figured it out from the way they look down on the average person on the island. It's not obvious because too many do the same. They fit in well with the haves and take from the have-nots.

"One day, and this was years ago, I was picking up dinner at the Fish Shack and saw the two of them. The husband, Charlie, left with a nod and a smile, and Tulsi followed. I just had that feeling, I don't know what it was exactly, but I looked over to Tulsi as she walked past another table. Cash had been left there with the bill, and Greg, who was down an employee and busy as all hell, hadn't had a chance to clear it. A second later, when I looked back to the table, the cash was gone and Tulsi was out the door. Did I see her take it? No, I was distracted, but I said something to Greg and mentioned it to Tolly. But there were no security cameras. Both Tolly and Greg let it go because she's an old woman, and they were both inclined to believe I was mistaken.

"They gave her a pass because of how she looked, you know, elderly and respectable. And that pissed me off. I had always figured there was a type of person I could tell was a criminal just by looking. Normally, I'd just let it go, but there was something about her, so I spent a few weeks digging, doing my homework on those two. They have places in Pennsylvania and New Mexico and divide their time between them. Scandal has followed them, but nothing has ever come of it. Charlie declared bankruptcy on a business while owing forty employees wages, simply closed his doors without a word and screwed them all out of their last paychecks.

"They frequently return items to stores after using them, too. Tulsi is really good at leaving complaints with retailers, restaurants, businesses, and she gets more free stuff because of it. As I said, they're takers, shitty human beings who would spit on the idea of brotherhood and never consider helping their fellow man. Unfortunately, that's not illegal."

Carmen said nothing. Billy Jo could see how on edge Gail was.

Just then, the door to the station opened, and in walked the interim mayor, Glen Vasquez. He had dark hair and was round in the middle, wearing blue jeans and a plaid shirt. Mark hung up the phone and stepped out of his office.

"Mayor Vasquez, wasn't expecting you," he said. Lacy had stepped out of the back room and was walking over to her desk.

"Can I have a minute, Chief?" Vasquez was direct, giving only a nod to Carmen and Gail, on whom he let his gaze linger for a second.

"Sure. My office?" Mark gestured with his thumb, and the mayor walked past Lacy and into the office. Mark gave him an odd look before walking over to them and resting his hand on Billy Jo's shoulder. Sometimes, by the way he touched her, she could feel how unsettled he was. "Carmen, I sent you a spreadsheet that Lisa Jenkins put together. Billy Jo will fill you in, but I just got off the phone with the local sheriff up in Port Angeles, where two kids in the system have apparently been missing for nine weeks. A police report number was issued, it seems, as a formality only. They were marked missing first and now runaways. No one is officially looking for them. Apparently, it's not a priority. Not their exact words, but I can read between the lines."

Billy Jo reached up and touched his hand, and he let his gaze linger on her as he said, "The spreadsheet Lisa has put together is impressive. The detail is alarming when you see it organized and cross-referenced like that. Any idiot could see there's a problem. It had to have taken her a while. You doing okay?" He was hovering again.

Billy Jo took in the mayor, who had stepped out of Mark's office, impatient and unsmiling, waiting for him. "Fine," she said. "Stop worrying. You'd better go see what he wants."

Mark gave her hand a squeeze before walking away. His hovering was something she didn't think she'd ever get used to. She listened to his door close.

"What's wrong?" Carmen asked. "Why is Mark so worried about you? Have I missed something? And what is this about missing kids?"

Billy Jo could hear the rumble of voices. The mayor sounded upset, but she couldn't make out a word of what was being said.

"And what is that about?" Carmen gestured to Mark's office quite sharply.

"I'd say it's about me," Gail said. "It'll have gotten around town by now that I'm suddenly working back in this office, and Mark is likely getting an earful about how I can't be here, that he needs to send me on my way because, well…" There it was, the haunted look that never seemed to leave Gail. "And Billy Jo fainted at work, Carmen. Mark is doing the overprotective husband thing. Lisa Jenkins, who has been a thorn in Billy Jo's side, has turned out to be a natural at digging through databases, doing the investigative grunt work of combing through files and putting all the details together so we can see the obvious that was buried in government bureaucracy, piles of paper and bullshit."

Carmen dragged her gaze from Gail back to Billy Jo. "You fainted?" she said. Out of all that, Carmen was stuck on the one thing Billy Jo didn't want to talk about.

"I was hungry, is all. Mark took me out for a burger after. And I hate to admit it, but Gail is right about Lisa. I have no idea how she pieced this together or how she figured it out, but I'll be the first to admit that maybe there's some use for her after all."

Mark's door opened with a clatter, and out walked the mayor, who stopped at the door as he pulled it open and called out, "You remember what I said, Chief." Then he headed out, and the door banged closed.

Gail was already reaching for her purse on the floor and setting it on the desk. She stood up and reached for her jacket over the back of the chair.

"What are you doing?" Mark asked as he walked over, shaking his head, looking really pissed.

"Mark, I'm a big girl," Gail said. "I know good and well what Vasquez wanted, and that's for me not to be here. Don't worry. You need anything, I'll be at home. Probably better this way. Folks here aren't ready to look at me or forgive me."

"Sit down. You're not going anywhere," Mark said. Billy Jo had never heard him snap at Gail like that. "You're right that he wanted you gone, but I said no. He has no say in who I bring in. I reminded him that he's only interim mayor, and he's overstepping. He has no input in the law."

The phone was ringing in the background, and she vaguely heard Lacy answer.

"Besides, we're all hands on deck now," Mark continued. "I need you to stay on top of the residents of the island. You know them better than anyone. Carmen, this missing kids thing, I want you to head over to the DCFS office and work with Lisa to figure out what's going on."

"Chief, that was Shana," Lacy called out. "She said Walter has been parked outside her bar and won't leave."

Mark let out a heavy sigh and dragged his hand over the back of his neck. "Okay, tell her I'm on my way," he said. He was walking back into his office, and it seemed everyone had their marching orders. Then there was Billy Jo.

"Carmen, I'll catch a ride with you," she said. "May as well go back to work…"

"No, you're with me," Mark said rather sharply as he walked back out of his office, pulling his jean jacket on over his holstered gun. "Lucky, you too. Come, on boy."

Billy Jo pushed herself out of the chair and felt everyone watching her as she strode over to where Mark had already reached for her jacket and was holding it up. "Mark, I have work to do," she said.

"Humor me. Besides, I need to talk to you."

She let him help her on with her coat, and he lifted her hair over the back, something he'd never done. Even though she wanted to argue, because it was what she did, there was a second when she realized, by the way he ran his hand over her back, and his tone, that there could be something more to his concern.

He reached for her bag, and she took it from him and walked out the door he had opened for her. Lucky trotted past them down to the Jeep. As Mark pulled the door closed and they walked together, she turned to him.

"Okay, so what did the mayor really want?" she said.

Mark rested his hand on the front of the vehicle and

stood close to her. "He wants Gail out of here. Seems the town's phones are ringing off the hook because word has hit the streets that she's back. He asked if I lost my mind and needed a refresher on what Tolly Shephard was involved in, the pedo ring he was protecting. I reminded Vasquez that I was the one who uncovered it, and Gail is as much a victim as the people here are, and I stand by my decision. Gail stays, as she's assisting with details of an ongoing investigation." His blue eyes lingered on her with worry and the weight of everything.

"So he's going to drop it, Gail being here?"

Mark looked past her. His face told her there was more. "No. He told me to get rid of Gail or finding a new chief for this island will be on his docket. He may be the interim mayor, but he's related to half the island and holds a ton of weight. He can sway people with his opinion. Apparently, he also received a call from Tulsi and Charlie's son about the squabble. His words, not mine. He ordered me to let it go, because she didn't mean any harm, and Merv has no idea the trouble that could come down on him."

"And you told him what?"

He walked around her and pulled her door open so she could climb in, which was something he just didn't do. Boy, he really was off. "What do you think? I told him to go to hell, and if he wants directions, I'll give them to him."

Twelve

The parking lot was half full and the sun starting to set as Mark parked off to the side and turned off the Jeep. "I don't see him," he said.

"Over there," said Billy Jo. "A white BMW with a man sitting inside, likely him?"

He found himself looking over to his wife, wondering why he was so unsettled and why she hadn't told him to knock it off. She was being far too reasonable. "You doing okay?" he said.

She pulled in a breath and let it out. "I'm fine, Mark. You need to stop hovering and worrying. You should go find out what he wants. I'll go and see Shana, let her know you're here, and she can come out and talk with you."

He let his gaze linger on her, then opened his door and stepped out. As he gave it a shove closed, Billy Jo was already out and walking to the bar. She knew him too well.

He just stood there for a minute until she was inside, unable to shake the need to know she was okay. Then he started over to the BMW parked beside a pickup, walking slow and steady, taking in everything until he was standing behind the vehicle. The plates, he noted, were from Vermont. The driver's door popped open, and out stepped Walter, wearing the same brown coat and blue jeans.

"What are you doing here, Walter?" Mark said. The man gave nothing away as he glanced to the door of the bar and back to Mark. Mark couldn't shake the thought that Walter had been poking around in his past. Just who the hell was he?

"Could ask the same of you, Chief. You following me? Seems our crossing paths too many times today is deliberate on your part."

The door to the bar opened, and laughter trailed out. Walter looked over to it, and Mark sensed more than anything how on edge the man was. Two women walked out and over to an old minivan.

"You're a little paranoid, there, Walter," Mark said. "Shana called because she doesn't want you sitting out in the parking lot. So, again, I'm going to ask you what you're doing here. Why are you sitting here? And if you ever threaten me or my wife again…"

"I didn't threaten you." Walter cut Mark off rather sharply, looking right at him, not cowering.

"Really? What do you call it, then, digging into my past, talking about our pets, our house, and a nest of snakes? I'm not an idiot. I know when someone is trying to warn me off. You should also know, with all your digging on me, that I don't scare easily. So what are you really doing here? Because Shana has made it clear she doesn't want you here."

The door of the bar squeaked open again.

"Get out of here now! I do not want you parked out here or showing up here anymore!" Shana yelled, storming right over to Walter. Billy Jo took her time walking over behind her. In Shana's voice, all Mark could hear was a woman who had been pushed too far.

"Look, I just want to talk to you, Shana," Walter said. "A moment alone to sit and talk. I don't think I'm being unreasonable, asking."

"Unreasonable?" Shana really leaned in and took another step toward him. "No, you showed up here with some bullshit story about making amends, but it's too late. Too many years have passed since you walked out. Good riddance, as far as I'm concerned. I'm fine. We're fine. I told you that already. And I'm not dealing with this paranoid shit of yours. You were pissed at me, thinking I sent the chief to your doorstep? Well, here he is. Let's get it out on the table."

Mark knew that was his cue. "Walter, Shana did not send me to your house. I already told you I want to know who's living on this island. You're new here, and you've never really given me a good reason why you moved back. Shana said you worked for some charity. You still working for them? How is it you can buy a place worth over twelve million? Didn't know you can make that kind of money working for a charity."

Shana hesitated, dragging her gaze from Mark to Walter. Evidently, she hadn't known.

"How is any of that your business, Chief?" Walter said. "Seems you're overstepping a bit."

He was hiding something, a lot of things.

"No, I don't think so," Mark said.

"You bought a twelve-million-dollar property?" Shana leaned in and made a rude noise, and Mark thought she swore under her breath.

"Look, I cashed everything in and bought the place because I want to be close to Haley. Where is she, anyway?

I haven't seen my daughter, and I want to. You're here working at a bar, so who is watching my daughter?"

Shana shook her finger at him. "You do not get to do that, showing up here and suddenly playing the concerned father. Haley is fine, I told you that already, and she has no idea who you are."

"You didn't answer me. Where is she?" he demanded. This was now turning into a personal situation that could pose a problem for Shana.

She gestured sharply, frustrated. "You just don't stop! Haley is fine. She's with my mom until I'm done here."

"I want to see her."

Shana was already shaking her head, and Mark could see he was dealing with two personalities that wouldn't bend. "No," she said. "She doesn't know you. You're out of her life, you stay out of her life. I'm not telling you again. Get the hell out of here, and don't come back. And this time I did call the chief on you, because I'm not having you sitting out here in the parking lot. It's creepy! Go back to your twelve-million-dollar property and stay the hell out of my life. Chief, get him out of here."

Mark nodded. "Walter, you heard Shana. You need to leave and not come back. She doesn't want you here."

The way Walter's mouth tightened, he seemed ready to pop off. "We're not done here, Shana," he said, then shook his head, pulled open the door of his BMW and climbed in, and started it up. He backed out and skidded his tires, sending gravel flying, and pulled onto the road.

Mark had realized something was going on here, something that could become a problem. He glanced over to Billy Jo, who was standing just behind Shana, and knew she had likely picked up more about Walter than even he had.

"You can file a formal complaint against him," he told

Shana, "and I can hit him with a trespass ticket and bar him from coming here, if you want. Not sure how much good that will do, though."

Shana shook her head. "No, don't bother. That will just piss him off. What the hell does he want, showing up here? He wants something, nursing a beer that he hates. I don't get him. Geez, maybe I never really knew him. Seriously, he bought a twelve-million-dollar property?"

Evidently, she had no idea of her husband's wealth, something else Mark needed to look into. At the same time, Walter had a reason to be there. But what that reason was, he didn't know.

"So you have no idea why he's here?" he said.

Shana shook her head again. "I told you yesterday, Chief, when you dropped by, that I have no idea. Why now? When he left, he just left, and him walking the way he did…" She gave her head a shake and pulled in a heavy breath. "Now I'm wishing I hadn't said anything to Lacy. Look what's been stirred up. I have a good life, and it doesn't include him. He feels bad for walking out, but I told him that's on him. I was past it long ago and moved on. The slow pace over here isn't for him. It's not his lifestyle. He'll get bored and move on to some new project, hopefully sooner rather than later, before he hurts my business or chases any of my customers away."

The door squeaked open. "Shana, the keg is empty," one of the workers called out, a young man with dark hair. "Need you in here so I can grab another from the back shed."

Shana lifted her hand. "Thanks, Tyler. On my way in." She turned back to Mark. "Thanks again for showing up, Chief. Sorry to be so heated. He just knows how to push my buttons."

"I'll drop by and pay him a visit, make sure he understands to leave you alone," Mark said.

Shana took a step around Billy Jo and then stopped. "Oh, and, Chief, when you do have a word with him, tell him I don't want his friends here, either."

"Friends?" he said.

Shana was already at the door. She stepped back, an odd look on her face. "Yeah, some friend of his was here earlier, asking a bunch of questions."

Billy Jo dragged her gaze from Shana over to him.

"Who was this friend, and what kind of questions was he asking?" Mark said.

Shana glanced back to the door. "I have no idea what his name was. Didn't ask. But he seemed far too interested in Haley, the last time we'd seen Walter, how we met… stupid stuff. So please tell Walter to tell his friends to stay the hell out of my bar."

Then she pulled open the door. The noise and the jukebox echoed out. Billy Jo stepped down and was walking his way.

"What do you make of all this?" she said.

Mark found himself looking at the parking lot and the road. The sun had gone down. "Walter has suddenly moved back to the island after leaving years ago, divorcing his wife, and leaving her with nothing, no support for his daughter. Yet now he buys a twelve-million-dollar property, says he wants to make amends? Okay, maybe he had a moment and realized he was an asshole, but what I find odd is that he greeted us with a shotgun as if he was expecting trouble. Now he's sitting in Shana's parking lot, and a friend of his showed up here. I don't know what to make of it. There's no such thing as a coincidence, and I just have a feeling about Walter that I can't shake, like there's something more going on."

Billy Jo pulled her arms across her chest and glanced to the door of the bar, then back to Mark. "Yeah, I think so too. What are you going to do?"

He slid his arm over her shoulders and started walking over to the Jeep, where he pulled open the passenger door for her. "I'm going to have Gail dig into Walter, his business, his friends, his life, and his bank account. And then I'm going to pay him another visit."

Billy Jo climbed in, and Mark stood there for a minute, looking at the parking lot and the rundown bar, its neon sign half burned out.

"What I can't figure out is how a man could just walk away from his family and leave them with nothing," he said. "None of this makes any sense."

She pressed a hand to his chest, a touch that settled him. He slid his hand over hers and leaned in to press a kiss to her lips.

"You'll figure it out, Mark," she said. "That's what I love about you: You don't walk away from a problem." There was that smile of hers he loved.

"I love you," he said, then pressed a kiss to her lips again.

He stepped back and shut her door. She was right about one thing. He intended to find out exactly what Walter Crandall wanted, what he was thinking, and what the real reason was for him being there.

Thirteen

Billy Jo felt a touch on her shoulder and jumped, realizing she must have dozed off in the bath.

"Hey, don't fall asleep in here," Mark said.

She blinked. The water had cooled.

"I have to go. Just got a call from the Dog and Whistle. Shana's mom called there about Haley. Shana never picked her up, and she's not answering her phone, but the staff said she left hours ago." Mark was in his jean jacket, likely one step out the door.

"I'll come with you." She scooted up and unplugged the bathtub.

"No, you're tired. You should just get some sleep. Don't wait up. I don't know how long I'll be." He held out a towel for her as she climbed out of the bath, his hand lingering a second as she took it. Then he was back in their bedroom.

She quickly dried herself off. "I just had a nap in the tub. I'm fine."

He was already pulling his gun from the safe in the closet. He flicked his gaze to her as she pulled open her drawer, retrieved a clean pair of underwear, and slipped them on, then shrugged on a black hoody and a matching pair of sweats.

"Would rather you didn't," he said, going overprotective again, as he holstered his gun after checking the rounds.

"I'm still coming. You think it was Walter?"

Mark pulled in a heavy breath and ran his hand impatiently over his face. Billy Jo sat on the edge of the bed and pulled on a pair of socks. One look in the dresser mirror and she could see her hair was a mess, so she pulled the brush through it before starting out of the bedroom. She realized Mark wasn't arguing as he followed behind her.

"Could be," he said. "I called Carmen and asked her to take a run over to Shana's. It seems like one big distraction. Can't figure out why, though. Lucky, stay."

Billy Jo was already at the front door, pulling on her sneakers, and Mark reached for her coat in the closet and held it out for her. She slipped it on, and he pulled the door open, impatient, distracted, gesturing for her to hurry. Lucky only stood there, his tail wagging.

Mark's cell phone rang while he was pulling the door closed behind them and shoving his key in the deadbolt to lock it, the cat and dog both inside. "Yeah," he said. "Carmen, is she there?" He was walking to the Jeep and gesturing for her to get in. "No, I'll head over to him. You go to the mother's," he said, then hung up.

Billy Jo climbed in, and Mark was already behind the wheel, the engine started, and backing up before she had her seatbelt on. "What was that about?" she said. It was dark, and the clock on the dash flashed after eleven. She'd really dozed off.

"Shana's house is dark. Her car isn't there, and no answer. Told Carmen to go over to the mother's house."

"You think she's at Walter's?"

He shrugged and pulled his seatbelt on as he drove, giving the Jeep gas, going faster than he normally would. "No idea, but likely," he said. He became really quiet when he was thinking and holding on to something.

"What are you thinking, Mark? 'Cause I know you've carried the weight of this island, and I've only added to it now with the missing kids. I know your feelings about Walter, that something about him isn't right. I was watching Shana outside the bar, and when you brought up the house he bought for twelve million, she was thrown completely. She didn't expect that. Frankly, I'm having a hard time understanding. He has that kind of money, yet her bar is in need of repair. She built that business herself. It has me wondering a lot of things about him and why he's back here now."

Mark flicked his high-beams on after passing a car that was driving the speed limit. He let out a heavy sigh. "Yeah, I figured as much. What is he doing, showing up here after he walked away the way he did? And then sitting outside in his car? Does he want to talk to her, or is he just watching her? And who is this friend who stopped by her bar? God damn the secrets and lies that seem to show up here."

Her husband couldn't hide how unsettled he was, and she realized she didn't have the right words to comfort him. But then, there were times when words meant nothing, so she reached over and touched his arm, feeling the tension.

"I'll go see a doctor tomorrow," she said.

He glanced her way and sighed as if she'd just taken some weight off his shoulders. At least she could do that much. "Should I ask why the change of heart or just say nothing?" He knew her too well.

She pulled her hand away, but he reached over and

gave it another squeeze. "Just for the record, I'm fine," she said. "I'm doing it only to give you some peace of mind."

He glanced back to the road as he pulled his hand away and geared down. They had reached Walter's place, and maybe he knew not to say anything else as he pulled down the long driveway. The trees on both sides cast shadows. She took in the large house, the lights on and an old Subaru parked in front.

"Well, damn. Pretty sure that's Shana's car," she said.

Mark pulled up and parked behind it, then looked over to her. "If I ask you to wait in the Jeep…"

She shook her head as she opened her door. "Not going to happen."

He only nodded, stepped out, and closed the door, and she walked around to join him. "Stay behind me."

"You know I will."

He looked at her in the dark and held out his hand, and she slid hers in it. He walked carefully, looking around the way he did. When the front door opened, Mark pulled away, his hand going automatically to his holstered gun.

"Chief, what the fuck now?" Walter was in the doorway, the light around him.

"Is Shana here?" Mark's other hand had gone out to her, and she knew he needed her to stay behind him.

Walter lifted his hand and stepped back. "Yeah, she's here."

"Well, I need to see her."

Walter gestured inside. Mark hesitated a second, then went in first, Billy Jo behind him. Walter's gaze flicked to her for a second, an edge in his brown eyes.

"Shana," was all Walter said. Then Billy Jo heard footsteps, and Shana appeared, wearing the same black t-shirt and blue jeans she had worn earlier, sock-footed.

"What's going on?" she said. "Chief, why are you here?"

"That's exactly what I'd like to know," Walter said, stepping around Mark and over to her.

Billy Jo glanced to the living room, where the dog sat in front of a crackling fireplace.

"Got a call from the bar," Mark said. "Your mother is looking for you, apparently. You didn't pick up Haley, and she's been trying to call you, but you're not answering your cell."

Walter shook his head.

Shana hurried over to the sofa table and pulled a cell phone from a brown purse. "Damn, it's dead," she said. "Walter, I need to use your phone."

He gestured and said, "In the kitchen," then let out a heavy sigh of frustration.

Billy Jo took another second to really observe how nice the place was, the windows, the furnishings, the high ceiling. Silence fell between Walter and Mark.

"No, I'm so sorry, Mom," Shana was saying. "My phone was dead. Look, I'm on my way home…" She was walking back into the room, the phone to her ear. Then she hung up, appearing a little out of sorts. "Walter, I have to go get Haley. Chief, sorry you had to come out. I feel like a fool. It seems everyone is overreacting." She reached for her coat, which had been tossed over the arm of the sofa.

"I'll walk out with you, Shana," Billy Jo said, glancing over to Mark and back to her.

"Sure."

"I'll be out in a minute," Mark said. "I want to have a word with Walter."

Shana shook her head, her expression alarmed, then walked around Billy Jo to pull on her sneakers and open the door. Billy Jo glanced back to Mark, who gave nothing away in his expression. She followed Shana out to find she was already at her car, fishing out her keys.

"Shana, everything all right?" Billy Jo said. The door to the house had closed, and the outside light was on.

Shana leaned against her car and pressed a hand to her face. "Yeah, fine. Just, can you believe this? I don't get him. I was devastated when he walked out, but I pulled it together and didn't let myself wallow too long. It was the way he cut it off that bothered me. Like it had been nothing. He didn't want to hear from me. He was just gone. Never heard from him about Haley. Honestly, I can't remember the last time he crossed my mind before he walked into my bar a few days ago, wanting to make amends. Like, what the fuck is this, this house? He always had money, but tossing twelve million at a house?" She was thrown, her lips firming as she went silent.

"It's a question, for sure," Billy Jo said.

"Where did he get the money, and who is he?" Shana said. "He's got a dog, but he hates animals, or he did when we were together. He hates beer, all beer, yet he sat in my bar and nursed a cheap draft. Who the hell is this, and why was he sitting outside my bar, waiting to talk to me?"

"So you came out here to him?" Billy Jo said, feeling the chill.

Shana was holding her keys, shaking her head. "Yeah, I did. I asked him what he was up to. You should have seen his reaction when I told him to keep his friends out of my bar," she said. "Look, I've got to go. My mom wants to go to bed, and I need to get Haley." She was already at her driver's door and had pulled it open.

"Shana, wait. What do you mean, his reaction about his friend? What's that about?"

Shana rested her arm on the open door and glanced

back to the house. "He freaked, demanded a name. I didn't get one, so then he was furious, wanting a description. I don't know what it was about. I asked him who it was. He rarely freaks out or gets scared, but I know when he is. He told me to call him if the guy showed up again, then started in on some bullshit about wanting me and Haley to move in here with him. I laughed in his face, then realized he was serious. So I'm a little rattled. I don't know what the fuck is going on or what shit he's brought to my doorstep. I told him to leave, go back to Vermont, back to his life, his job, his whatever…and you know what he said?"

Billy Jo knew she was frowning. She didn't look away. "I don't know, Shana. You'll have to tell me."

"He said he doesn't have a job anymore. He quit. So I asked him, what the hell? The way he looked at me, I had a feeling I didn't want to know. I asked him what he had done, and instead of denying it, he decided to go all philosophical, saying there were lines even he wouldn't cross. That was all I got before you pulled in. Now I've got to go…" She moved to get in her car.

"Wait, Shana, didn't he work for some charity?"

She slid behind the wheel, and Billy Jo rested her hand on the frame of the door, seeing how rushed and thrown she was. "Sure, some big nonprofit. All I know is he said it involved kids, a lot of kids, and that was only one part of the organization. He said he stumbled across something he wasn't supposed to see—missing kids, drug trials… But those people are untouchable. I told him I didn't want to know anymore. Now, Billy Jo, I've really got to go."

Billy Jo stepped back, and Shana closed her door, started up her car, and pulled away. As Billy Jo glanced back to Walter's house, she realized her feeling of being on edge always came down to protecting kids.

Billy Jo was walking back to the house, illuminated by the taillights as Shana drove away. In front of Mark, Walter had pulled his arms over his chest, unrest simmering in his brown eyes.

"Chief, I already told you it's time for you to go," he said. "You did your due diligence and found Shana for her worried mama, and now she's on her way home, so you can skedaddle as well."

Mark reached for the door and pulled it open so Billy Jo could walk in. "Not so fast," he said. "I want to know what the hell's going on here. Shana was fit to be tied and didn't want you in her life. In fact, she called me at the station because you were parked outside her bar. What I saw was a man who either was stalking his ex-wife or was worried about her. So which was it? Again, it comes down to the question of why you're really here, Walter."

The door clicked closed, and he glanced back at Billy Jo, whose eyes said there was something on her mind. Walter lifted both hands in the air and took a step down into the living room. He walked over to the dog, ran his hand over its head, and shoved another piece of wood on the fire, which crackled. Billy Jo slid a hand over Mark's arm.

"You know, Chief," Walter said, "sometime a man makes mistakes. He wakes up one morning and realizes the choices he made to protect his family were the wrong ones. I never said I never cared, but the fact of the matter is that this is between me and Shana, not me and the chief of police on the island."

Mark glanced down to Billy Jo when she ran her other hand over his arm. "Everything okay?" he said.

She angled her head. "Shana said a few things you may want to ask Walter about," she said, loud enough for him to hear. "He seemed concerned about this friend of his and the job he just quit."

Walter was watching them, sitting on the fireplace hearth, and pulled his arms across his chest. Mark knew he was frowning.

"Walter, do you mind if I ask you a question?" Billy Jo said.

"You can always ask, but I'm not saying I'll answer."

Billy Jo pointed her thumb at the door behind her. "Just had an interesting conversation with Shana. You haven't been too forthcoming with Mark. I wonder if you want to talk about the charity you worked for and what it had to do with kids. Shana's exact words were that you stumbled across something involving missing kids and drug trials. Who was it you worked for, again?"

Mark wanted to pull Billy Jo aside. "What are you talking about?" he said to his wife.

She frowned and gestured outside again. "Shana was upset, angry, thrown, pissed, maybe all of the above. Said Walter wanted her and Haley to move in with him, as if he's expecting trouble."

Mark dragged his gaze over to Walter, who reached down and ran his hand over his dog again.

"You know, I never allowed myself to have a pet, not when Shana and I were together," Walter said. "She wanted one, but I told her I didn't like dogs or cats. The real reason was that I saw firsthand what they did to animals in the name of science. The horror of hearing them squeal… Yes, science. In those labs, they experiment, supposedly for the betterment of mankind. People are okay with that because they're told we have to experiment to save lives. I can tell by your face you have no idea what I'm talking about."

Mark only shrugged, though Billy Jo stilled and gripped his arm. "I'm not sure what this has to do with missing kids or your worry for Shana," he said. "Who is this friend she was talking about?"

Walter let out a heavy sigh but didn't stand up. "Not a friend. Sounds like someone delivering a message, you know, to make sure I'm not talking."

There it was again, that uneasy feeling that was Mark's unwelcome friend. "What the fuck are you involved in, Walter?" He looked down at Billy Jo. "She really said that?"

"And then some," Billy Jo said. "She was spooked. What did your charity have to do with missing kids? What kids?"

For a moment, Mark wondered whether Walter would pull the "Talk to my lawyer" card again.

"You have any idea how large charities work?" Walter glanced over to Billy Jo, then back to Mark. He suddenly seemed calm, too calm.

"You mean like collecting donations and giving money to those in need?" Mark said.

Walter let out a rough laugh. "Yeah, as too many

believe. Crash course, Chief? Charities and nonprofits are created to funnel cash, large amounts of cash. They receive federal grants and pledges from the public, as well as tax dollars and foreign dollars, which they funnel through to businesses and corporations. The foundation I worked for, the Wilson Foundation, was founded by the family—yes, the former head of state, his wife, and his kids. I worked with them and their mega-charity. The bulk of their windfall goes to administration, salaries, travel, and huge bonuses, enormous payouts to family friends who own the corporations that own everything, and the Wilson family has shares in those same corporations." He gestured to Mark, who wasn't sure he'd heard him right.

Walter sighed. "Okay, Chief, I'm going to say this only once, and this is a very simplistic overview, but when you see how it's all connected, it will blow your fucking mind. They funnel money to two of the largest asset-holding companies in the world. The power of these two companies is beyond your imagination, because they own stocks in nearly every large company. Along with the stocks of their investors, they create a monopoly the average person will never get their head around. I'm talking every industry.

"Think of it this way, Chief. The richest families in the world own all this. It's a funnel through big pharma, big tech, media, entertainment, the food industry, and yes, banking. Even government agencies are in fact owned by this group. And just to be clear, there isn't a chance in hell I'm going to talk to you about what I saw or give you names, because one, you wouldn't believe me, and two, I'd be dead. Yeah, missing kids. I mean, look at you, Billy Jo, a social worker, and you have no fucking idea of the criminal organization you work for. How many kids disappear every year, and no one is looking for them? You have any idea how they're tracked once they're in the system?"

Mark couldn't pull his gaze. Billy Jo hissed, and her fingers dug into his arm.

"You know anything about kids in the system disappearing?" Billy Jo snapped. "More than one hundred thousand kids, and no one is looking for them?"

Walter shook his head. "You really think that's all there is? You can add another zero to that number. You have no idea. Animals, kids, all that sick shit is about money. You want to know how they can operate in the shadows? It's because they own your politicians, and the judges. They compromise them, groom them, and place them, and they're really good at that. I wish to hell I could unsee everything I've seen. I wish I could go back to that day twenty years ago when I walked through the front door of the charity for my job interview and instead do anything else—fishing, sailing, working as a mechanic.

"But you can't go back. And you will only ever see what they want you to see. I would know. I handled all the marketing, whatever the narrative had to be, whatever the media had to put out, whatever the people needed to believe. People will never believe the government could be part of anything so heinous. But to try to bring them down is as good as asking for a bullet in the back of your head or a visit from some sheriff or federal agent who will book you on charges they've made sure will stick. More than likely, I'd disappear and never be found."

Walter clasped his hands but released them when his dog looked up at him again. "You have any idea how many nights I wake up in a cold sweat? There isn't a damn thing I can do but read up on everything. Know your enemy. It has always been about money. Did you know that there are basically around four hundred drugs give or take that actually work, and the rest are created, hundreds of thousands, basically for money and profit?

"They keep the sick sicker and the sicker one step from the grave. They tell the doctors which drugs to push. They own the medical schools, so they teach them what they want them to know. And every time they need a drug trial, they use the kids in the system, after the animals, in the most horrific cruel ways. If you knew, you'd never sleep again. Hospitals get funding, doctors get money, and no one says anything. The money flows through all of it.

"Property is bought up. Everything is slowly being controlled. I left Shana and walked away because I saw some of the sick shit, how the charity had its hands in so many pots. I was promoted into my position when the former deputy head of marketing had an unfortunate accident. He and his family were gunned down along with five other people at an Indian restaurant. The media said it was a mentally unstable man who hated Muslims, but that was the narrative. Every news station told the same story.

"But Ed himself had mailed me a letter, dated three months earlier, that said if something happened to him, it was because he knew too much and had become a liability. I think he made a deal and developed a conscience. I left because I wasn't going to watch as Shana and Haley suffered the same fate. Sure, I did it in the most asshole of ways, leaving her with nothing, because I needed all the executives and people watching me to believe she meant nothing to me. Divorcing her, cutting her out and off, was the only way I could make sure I had no one they would use against me. These are not people with a conscience…"

Walter's phone had started ringing, and he stood and walked over to it. "Excuse me a moment," was all he said before he picked it up and turned from them, saying, "Hello?"

Billy Jo tapped his arm. "Mark, what the hell?" she said in a low voice.

"I understand," Walter said, then hung up and set the phone back in the cradle. He took a moment before turning around with an odd look on his face.

Just then, Mark's cell phone started ringing.

"Shit," he said as he saw Carmen's name on the screen. "What is it?"

"We got a problem, Chief. A group of residents are outside Gail's house, one with a torch, literally threatening to burn her out. They want her off the island."

He thought his eyes bugged out. He gave a sharp glance to Billy Jo. "On my way," he said. "Get over there now."

"Almost there," Carmen said.

He hung up. "We've got to go," he said. "Gail has some visitors, and there could be some bloodshed." He reached for the door. "Walter, I've got an emergency."

"Go, Chief," Walter said. "I've told you all I'm going to. It's late. I'm going to call it a night."

Billy Jo was already out the door, and Mark was right behind her.

"I'll call you tomorrow," he said. "We're not done here." Then he was running to his Jeep and sliding behind the wheel. He looked back to see Walter closing the door. He didn't know how to wrap his head around what had basically been dumped in his lap.

"Mark, I'm really scared," Billy Jo said. He'd never heard her talk that way.

"I know. Shit, one disaster at a time, though." He spun his Jeep around, giving it gas as he pulled his seatbelt on.

"Kids and animals," Billy Jo whispered under her breath and glanced out the passenger window.

"We'll figure it out, I promise you."

She glanced over to him. "Any chance he's lying?"

For a moment, he considered telling her what she wanted to hear. He shook his head.

"Yeah," she said. "Just what I thought."

He glanced over to his wife again as he pulled onto the main road, feeling as if there were a bigger monster out there than he knew, one he didn't have a chance in hell of bringing down.

Fifteen

Cars were parked all along the side of the road on the way to Gail's house, traffic the likes of which Billy Jo had never seen. A siren wailed in the distance from Carmen's cruiser, its lights flashing and driver's door open.

Mark drove across the once nice lawn because a pickup was now parked across the driveway, blocking it. Billy Jo pressed her hand to the door and vaguely heard Mark swear at the sight. The siren blasted again. In front of the house was a mob of thirty, maybe forty people with a torch and signs. Someone was holding a stick with a noose hanging from it.

"For fuck's sake," Mark muttered. "You stay here and lock the doors."

He was out of the Jeep, his gun out of its holster, and he fired it in the air and shouted, "What the hell is going on here? Get back now!"

Billy Jo had never heard Mark shout like that. The crowd was crazed. Who were these people? She tried to see someone, anyone she knew. She realized a news camera was there and journalists, too. How the hell had that happened? The white front door to Gail's house was closed, but two men stood by it, and she thought they were trying to kick it in. It had been spraypainted in red with some insignia she couldn't make out.

Mark moved into the shouting crowd. It seemed everyone had lost their fucking minds, and Mark was right in the middle of it. If this went sideways, there were too many of them against him. She felt pure terror at the thought of him getting hurt.

She pulled open her door and stepped out, and she spotted one of the part-time medics. What was his name…Ryan? He had on a hat, and she had to really look to recognize him. Who was the woman with him? Someone she'd seen on the island, but she didn't know her name. A camera was now on Mark, a photographer in the crowd, snapping photos. Two others were blocking Carmen. A confrontation, maybe?

Carmen shouted, and Billy Jo spotted Mark at the door to Gail's house, holding his badge in the air.

"You are all trespassing on private property," he yelled. "Get out of here now and go home! Anyone still here in the next ten seconds is under arrest. Put that damn torch out!"

Billy Jo shoved her hands in her pockets and took a step just behind the crowd. A woman with a sign was yelling, "Kill her! Burn her for the children!" She wore a black shirt, with dark hair, and Billy Jo had never seen her before.

"Can you believe this?" the woman said to her. There were a few men nearby, and women, with scarfs over their faces. "Have you got a sign?"

Billy Jo turned to the Jeep. She'd left the door open.

She was in her black coat and lifted her hood to cover her head. "No, where are the signs?"

"You were supposed to grab one from the pickup, over there," the woman said.

Billy Jo glanced over her shoulder. Amid the shouting, another gunshot was fired in the air. She ducked, and so did others.

"Fucking crazy cop!" the woman shouted. "He's going to kill someone. He'll be splashed all over the news, though. We'll fucking wreck his life. He'll wish he'd never shown up. Damn, this one was easy."

Billy Jo looked at the woman and just took in her surroundings. The people had a crazed energy that could catch anyone up in their madness, and she felt their hate simmering. What the hell was she talking about?

Glass shattered nearby. Billy Jo was trying to place the woman or anyone else there. She didn't see Ryan anymore. The news people were off to the side, cameras out. This was an absolute shitshow.

Someone was yelling, "Burn her out! Burn her out!" A few more started chanting.

"You from here?" Billy Jo said.

The woman gave her a passing glance. "No, came over on the ferry. Don't remember seeing you. They should have some good shots for the media. This will be great. Where did you head in from?"

Holy shit, what the hell was going on? She felt the anger pulse, and in that second, she realized the protest had been organized. "A small town just across the Nevada border," she said. "What about you?"

"Portland. Most of us are. You hear we're supposed to get a bonus on this one?"

Billy Jo was afraid to look over her shoulder. "How many locals you think are here?"

The woman shrugged. "One or two. A few of the neighbors. It was easy, you know, to fire up some of these angry snowflakes who don't have the balls to do anything. A few have joined in, but we'll be gone before the dust settles…"

A tall, lanky man walked over, young, dark. "Who is that?" he said and gestured to Billy Jo.

She had that feeling of being busted, her heart thudding. The crazed energy was like nothing she'd ever felt.

"She's from Nevada," the woman said. "No names, remember?"

She spotted Ryan again. He was on the other side of the crowd, saying something to another woman she'd never seen before. They were both looking her way, and then the woman, with brown hair pulled back under a ball cap, was walking toward her. Someone said something nearby, and people were suddenly stepping away from her, one and then another, disappearing in different directions.

"Time to go," someone said to a person in front of her. She looked around to see that Mark had two people cuffed and on the ground.

Now only a few protestors were left. A firetruck siren blasted, and she spotted its lights. The cameraman was gone, and so were the journalists.

Billy Jo slid off her hood and started over to Mark. He was pissed off. The windows of Gail's house were broken, the sputtering torch on the ground alongside a doll with a noose around its neck.

"I told you to stay in the Jeep," Mark snapped. He holstered his gun and dragged his gaze past her to see who was still there. "Carmen, stuff these two assholes in your car and book them for mischief, property damage, inciting a riot, and anything else you can think of."

Carmen gestured to the two men. Some of the firefighters had walked over, and Mark dragged his hand over his face again, which he did when he was dealing with something difficult. Billy Jo walked around the two cuffed men on the ground.

Mark was at the door. He fisted his hand and pounded. "Gail, it's Mark! Open up. Need to see if you're okay."

Billy Jo stepped up beside him, and he flicked his gaze to her, protective, angry, pissed. The deadbolt clicked, and then the door opened, slowly, just a bit, enough that Billy Jo could see tears and fear on the face of a woman who didn't deserve any of this.

"Are they gone?" Her voice was strained.

Mark pressed his hand to the door, pushing it open gently, and Gail stepped back. "Yeah, got two assholes arrested, but the rest are gone. You can't stay here. You hurt?"

Billy Jo rested a hand on Mark's arm, and his gaze shot right to her. He must have known what she needed to do, as he stepped back and let her step inside. The house was dark. Billy Jo flicked on the inside light.

"No, Mark, I'm not hurt," Gail said. "Scared the shit out of me. Mark, my neighbors wanted to burn me out. They smashed the windows at the side. I locked myself in the bathroom…"

Billy Jo took in the rifle leaning against the wall. Gail had an arsenal, everything Tolly had left behind. "Mark is right," she said. "You can't stay here. But they weren't your neighbors. I recognized Ryan, a part-time medic with the fire department, and maybe a couple others, but most of them aren't from here. They came in on the ferry. Jesus, Mark, I think someone organized this. There were news media, not from here, and a woman in the crowd said something to me. I think they were paid to do this."

Gail's hand was over her mouth, and the spooked look

in her eyes was back. Mark said nothing. His cell phone rang again.

"Jesus fucking Christ, what now?" He had the phone out and to his ear. "What? Lacy, slow down… No, I'll go. You go to the station. Carmen is bringing in two motherfuckers who were here, terrorizing Gail." Then Mark hung up and shut his eyes a second, pulling in a heavy breath.

"Mark, what is it?" Billy Jo said.

Mark didn't look at her, just gestured sharply to Gail and said, "Get your coat. You're coming with us." Then he reached for the rifle, checked to see whether it was loaded, flicked the safety on, and looked at Billy Jo. "We're heading over to Shana's. It's like this damn island is falling apart tonight. Lacy got a text from Shana, an odd text: 'The lemonade is burning.'"

Gail pulled a heavy brown sweater from the closet, and her eyes widened as she dragged her gaze over to Mark. "Did I miss something?"

"Apparently, Lacy and Shana have a code word," he said. "They watch each other's backs. If one is in trouble, she texts the other—"

"Not just Lacy and Shana," Gail said. "I know the code too, Mark, and a few others on the island do, as well. You get a code word, have a buddy. Lacy and Shana are two single women who've had trouble in their lives."

"Let's go," Mark said, then headed over to Billy Jo, stepping right in her space, those amazing blue eyes flickering with fire. "Next time I tell you to stay in the fucking Jeep, you stay in the fucking Jeep."

He reached for her hand and started out the door, looking right and left. Carmen had shoved the last of the two cuffed men in the back of her cruiser, and Mark called out to one of the firemen, "Board up the broken windows!"

Billy Jo didn't pull away from him, and Gail was right behind her. Mark moved the passenger seat forward so Gail could climb in the back, then stopped in front of Billy Jo before she could get in.

"You sure it was Ryan?" he said.

She nodded. "And he saw me."

Mark said nothing else. She slid in the passenger side, and as he closed the door, she felt Gail's hand on her shoulder. Mark slid the rifle on the floor in the back and got in, and Billy Jo couldn't shake the feeling that tonight, everything was heating up.

CHAPTER
Sixteen

"That's Walter's car," Billy Jo said, pointing to the BMW parked in the driveway of Shana's house, a small bungalow with too many trees hiding it from the road.

Mark turned off his headlights and pulled up in front of the mailbox. "I want you to stay in the Jeep," he said. "I need you to listen to me this time. This could be nothing, or…"

Or it could be something he didn't want anywhere near his wife, he thought. He felt her hand on his arm as he flicked off the overhead light before pulling open his door, considering surprise was the only thing he had on his side.

"Stop worrying about me," she said. "I'll wait here with Gail. You just watch your fucking back and don't do anything stupid."

Okay, so they were there with each other. He climbed out, glancing back to Gail and the rifle on the floor.

"We'll be fine, Mark," was all she said.

He closed the door quietly and made his way around the house, staying in the shadows of the yard as he moved to the side. The front door was closed, as were all the windows. He kept his back to the wall, quietly opening the small back gate, and spotted a hint of light from the back window. He thought he heard voices as he put his hand on the door, knowing it was likely locked. But the knob turned, and Mark pulled it open and slipped in, very aware of where he was stepping. He held the door until it closed without a sound.

"Again, I asked you who you talked to." It was a man's voice. Walter?

Mark angled his head, really listening. No, it was someone else. His gun was in his hand as he took in the three back steps. He pressed his back to the wall.

"I already told you, I talked to no one and she has nothing to do with this. Let her go."

"That's not how this works, Walter. You know that. A favor was expected. Walking away is not a right you have without giving something in return. You know too much. You had to know this would be coming, and they don't have enough on you to keep you in line…"

Mark took another step up, peering into an old boxy kitchen. He knew the voices were in the other room. A quick look around the corner and he spotted a man holding a gun to Walter's head. Walter was on his knees.

"Okay, you're right," he said. "I know about all the trafficking, the kids, the women, the drugs, the guns across the border and through the east coast ports. I know money is being funneled to S&P corporations and into the pockets of wealthy families. I know every illegal thing being done under the guise of charity. Over three thousand sheriffs in this country, and over half are owned and compromised. I know every investigation that has been shut down. I know Bob Wields, one of the new managing directors, sacrificed his five-year-old daughter to those sick fucks because they demanded it, for his new position. The manhunt for his missing little girl has turned up nothing. The sheriff in charge of the investigation made sure evidence pointed another way. Do I know what they did to her? I don't want to, because those sick fucks are the devil themselves.

"I know they've been in damage control since they took out Ed and his family. They're cleaning house, controlling the narrative and news cycle so the finger is always pointing somewhere else. Except they're panicking, and I saw the writing on the wall. My turn was coming, because they're fucking paranoid. Every person who knows too much or can't be compromised suddenly has an accident or commits suicide.

"But I have evidence for every secret they have, every dime they've laundered and funneled into the companies they own. And you have no idea where that evidence will go. Despite all the Feds you've compromised and the cops on your payroll, the media in your pockets, I know ones who aren't, two or three journalists who will get the truth out and cops who will find a way to prosecute. You have no idea who they are, but enough copies will be sent that the moment something happens to me or my family, every-thing will come crashing and burning down. They're already losing control, and they won't be able to walk. That's what will happen as soon as you kill me."

"Oh, I'm not going to kill you," the man said. "I'm going to make you watch what I do to your little girl first. Your ex-wife will be begging and pleading for you to stop me, to give me what I want. The screams will haunt you. Then I'll start on her and you will tell me where every copy is..."

Mark swung around the corner, his gun aimed, safety off, seeing Walter, the man aiming the gun right at him, and Shana against the wall, her nose and mouth bleeding, holding a little girl in her arms.

"Drop it, now!" he yelled.

The man flicked his gun to Mark and fired, but he ducked. Wood splintered above his head. Walter roared and lunged at the man's legs, and at the same time, Mark fired two shots into his chest, sending him back, blood oozing from his lips. Walter reached for the man's gun and held it up, about to fire at his head.

"Drop it, Walter, now!" Mark hurried in, ready to fire again, right behind Walter, who was still on his knees.

Walter let the gun fall to the ground just as Mark heard the back door click open again.

"Mark!" Billy Jo cried out. Gail was behind her, pointing the rifle.

Mark took a second and dragged his gaze to the man on the floor, the life having seeped out of him. He knew when someone was dead.

"I told you to stay in the Jeep," Mark snapped, not turning around. He reached for the gun on the ground. Walter was over by Shana on the floor, holding her and his daughter, crying silently. Mark shoved the gun in the waistband of his jeans and kicked the foot of the dead man.

"And I told you not to do anything stupid," Billy Jo said. "We heard shooting. You have any idea what it did to me to hear that, not knowing if you were hurt? Is he dead?"

Mark glanced back to Billy Jo, then to Walter, who was now standing, holding the little girl, and Shana, who wiped her mouth. Mark leaned down and reached for the man's wrist, but there was no pulse. "Yeah," he said. "Who is this, Walter?" Even to his own ears, he sounded calm, but he was anything but.

"Not sure, exactly," Walter said. "One of many who cleans up for the company."

"He broke my nose," Shana said. Gail had flicked the safety on the rifle, and Billy Jo walked around Mark, over to Shana.

"Let me see," she said. Walter was holding his little girl tight. She had his eyes, Mark realized. Gail had her cell phone out and was calling someone.

Walter put the little girl down. "Go on over to Mommy," was all he said, and Shana and Billy Jo moved into the kitchen, the little girl with them. Walter pulled his arms across his chest.

"What the fuck is this, Walter?" Mark said. "What you said about evidence, trafficking, drugs…you're talking racketeering. Wait, who called you?"

Walter ran his tongue over his bottom lip. "You already know. He was just telling me my options, which were to get my ass over here."

"So if I hadn't shown up…"

"Shana and I would have been discovered dead, and Haley would have been gone. Evidence would have been planted to make it look like I killed Shana and then myself. He was only one man, and I think you already know his body will never be claimed. It was a clean shoot. This will go nowhere. You have a spooked look on your face, Chief, and you should. You have no idea the reach these people have. They'll send someone else after Shana, Haley, and me. We're going to have to disappear, and the only way we can do that, Chief, is if the world believes we're dead."

Gail hung up her cell phone and turned to Mark, looking as if the night had kicked the shit out of her, adding another ten years to her. "Carmen is on her way," she said.

Mark took in Walter, the man on the floor, and the

voice of the woman he loved in the kitchen. "Call her back. Tell her I got this. She needs to deal with those assholes who showed up at your place."

Gail flicked her gaze from Walter to Mark as if she knew something was up. "Where should I tell her I am?"

He considered what he was doing for a moment. "You tell her you're here," he said. He didn't miss the surprise in her expression before she raised her cell phone again and stepped into the kitchen. Mark took in the body on the floor. "How deep does this go?"

"Deeper than you can handle," Walter said. "You have any idea how many parents are willing to sell their kids? You think politicians really get elected? People believe what they want them to, and charity is never just charity. The people who blow the whistle on these high-profile pedophiles tend to disappear, have accidents, or kill themselves. And you can't just run and hide, because they will find you."

Mark ran his hand over his face.

Billy Jo appeared in the doorway, holding a bloody cloth. "Shana should go to the hospital," she said. "I think her nose is broken."

Walter didn't pull his gaze from Mark as he said, "Hospitals have records. She'll be dead before the night's over."

"You make it sound like everyone is bought and compromised," Mark said.

Walter said nothing for a moment, then shook his head and glanced back to Billy Jo, who was standing there, watching. "No, not everyone, but the right ones have been bought. They have compliance from sitting judges, politicians, and the ruling elite. They've been doing this a really long time. You know how they see you and me and the average person? As slaves. Only our chains now are our massive debt, which is theirs."

"I don't know what you're suggesting," Mark said. He knew Billy Jo was still there, watching, listening, furious with him.

"I think you do," Walter said. Gail had appeared and was saying something to Billy Jo.

"Shana is going to need a doctor," Mark said.

"I know someone," Walter replied.

Gail walked his way. "Well, what are we doing here, boys?" was all she said, looking from Mark to Walter and back. "There are seven of us here, and one is dead. Your wife and Shana filled me in, Mark. So, again, what are we doing?"

Walter pulled his arms over his chest, and Mark took in a cut he hadn't noticed on his chin.

"You should get going," Mark said. "I'll handle it."

"They'll need bodies, or it will never be believed," Walter said.

Gail didn't look away. She had figured out what needed to happen. "You heard the chief, Walter. Get your family out of here. We've got this."

Walter let his gaze linger on her for a second. Then he stepped forward and held out his hand to Mark. "Thanks, Chief."

Mark shook his hand and watched as he walked into the kitchen.

Billy Jo was headed his way. "What the hell, Mark?"

He slid his arm around her, pulling her close. "I need you to trust me," he said, then pressed a kiss to the top of her head.

She frowned as she looked up. "You know I do."

"Good, because we're the only ones who are going to know what really happened here."

Billy Jo frowned again. "What are we doing, Mark?"

"We're saving a family."

Billy Jo sat in the Jeep, watching the flickering flames rip through Shana's house, knowing Walter was long gone with her and Haley. Sirens sounded in the distance just as Mark pulled open the door to the Jeep and Gail climbed in the back behind her, smelling of gasoline.

A boom rocked the Jeep just as Mark started it, and he pulled away from the curb just as a firetruck rounded the corner.

"You sure it will work?" Billy Jo said.

Gail reached forward and squeezed her shoulder. "It will be fine. The fire is hot enough. A gas leak will be blamed. After the fire department puts out the fire and finds the remains, Mark will be called in to investigate. Walter, Haley and Shana will be reported missing, their bodies not found. You should take a few days off, Billy Jo."

Mark said nothing as he turned the corner, giving the Jeep some gas and shifting gears to drive the speed limit, which he never did.

"How do you know this will work?" Billy Jo said.

Mark slid his hand over hers. She could feel the grit, and the scent of smoke lingered on him. "I'll make sure of it," he said, then squeezed her hand again. Damn, did she love him.

"Where are we going now?" she said.

He glanced over to her and then back to the road as he turned down their street. "We're going home," he replied.

And she knew what he meant: all three of them, Mark, Gail, and her.

Seventeen

It was three in the morning as Mark stood on the dock, taking in the flames flickering over the last pieces of the boat that had belonged to Walter, most of which had already sunk. The coast guard had a boat on the water, and he knew divers were underneath. He could hear shouting, voices, and the spotlight of the coastguard boat. He knew well the sounds of a search underway.

"They find anyone?" called out Carmen, who strode up in a heavy dark coat, her dark hair pulled back.

Mark shoved his hands in his jean jacket pockets. "Nope, no one," he said. "Not much left of the boat, and it's pretty deep out there. With the tide, who's to say whether anything will wash up and where? Who did you say called in the explosion? And you're sure they saw Shana and Haley on board?"

Carmen shrugged. "Not sure who called it in, but the call went straight to the coast guard. Whoever it was said they heard arguing between Shana and Walter and then saw her and Haley get on the boat. But she was here earlier, remember? Why would she and her daughter come back to get on a boat in the middle of the night with Walter? She was a really nice lady, tough as nails… Damn, Lacy is going to take this hard. They were friends. You think they'll find any remains? I just got off the phone with the fire chief about the body they found at Shana's, too. There's nothing left of the house. God damn, Chief. What the hell went on here tonight? And those two yahoos who were part of the group that terrorized Gail don't even live here. I have them locked up back at the station. I'm so tired of this shit. Is Gail okay?"

Mark didn't pull his gaze from the lights on the ocean. He knew they were wrapping it up. "She's fine. She's staying with us. We have room for her. So explain to me again what those two men said. And don't forget Ryan. You going to pick him up and find out his role in this?"

He stepped off the dock, and Carmen fell in beside him. Walter's massive property and house were lit up. He squeezed the folded envelope in his pocket, which had his name on it and had been left on the counter in the kitchen with a flash drive and a note that read, *This is one of many copies.* He had taken it before anyone else saw. Then there was the dog Walter had left.

"The two guys we arrested have no ID," Carmen said, frustrated. "They've said nothing and are demanding a call to their lawyer. Lacy is there at the station with them. I can pick up Ryan next, but I'm only one person, Chief, and I think the dead body at Shana's and this scene trumps a bunch of rioters."

Mark glanced up to the house to see two volunteers from the coast guard inside. "You find anything else here?" he asked Carmen.

She shook her head. "Nothing other than an emptied closet and drawers left open as if he packed in a hurry. He left his dog. Why would he leave his dog? I'll have Lacy call the shelter in the morning."

At least Mark could do something there to ease Carmen's stress. "No, I'll take the dog and handle that," he said. "I want you to pick up Ryan and let those two yahoos see you park him in a cell. There's nothing you can do here. Someone is going to start talking about who was behind the protest, terrorizing Gail. Those rioters weren't from here. Someone's paying them. I want to know who and why. I'll be right behind you."

For a second, he thought she was going to argue, but she didn't, just walked back up the hill. The coast guard pulled up to the dock soon after, and Mark walked back down and over to the lieutenant who had stepped off the boat along with one of the divers.

"Well, anything?" Mark said. The last of the wreckage had sunk, extinguishing the flames.

"No, we'll pick it up in the morning," the lieutenant said. "But it's unlikely we'll find anything. Looks like explosives. It's pretty deep, and the tide is pulling everything out, so the chance of recovering a body is small. Seems someone had an issue with him."

Mark let his gaze linger on the darkness of the ocean. "It does seem that way. Thanks, Lieutenant," was all he said. The two volunteers from the house walked past him to the waiting boat at the dock, and no one said anything else.

He waited a moment as the coast guard pulled away, then made his way back up to the house. His Jeep was parked out front, and Carmen's cruiser was gone. He opened the door and stepped inside to be greeted by the friendly lab he knew had been left for him. He bent down and ran his hand over the dog. "Well, Sarge, guess you're coming home with me."

He took in the blue collar the dog was wearing and the leash on the table by the front door. He hooked the leash and said, "Come on," then flicked off the lights in the living room and pulled open the door to lead the dog out, leaving the outside light on.

When he closed the door, he breathed in the quiet of the night, the darkness before the dawn, the silence before the birds started their song at four a.m. He pulled open his Jeep and put Sarge in back, then climbed in, feeling the weight of everything. Sometimes, it seemed the only way to protect someone was to find a way to be sure no one was looking for him.

THE SUN WAS COMING up when Mark arrived at the station to see that Carmen was pissed off and Lacy's desk was empty. The lab had immediately curled up in Lucky's dog bed in the corner.

"Well," Carmen said, "Ryan is in back, and he's lawyered up and is demanding a phone call. What do you want to do?"

Mark pulled out the thumb drive from his pocket and squeezed it, then unlocked his desk drawer and dropped it in there along with his car keys. "I'd say it's time to have a chat with them." He walked around his desk and held out his hand. "Key."

Carmen held out the key to the old cell doors, and Mark took it and headed for the two cells in back. He stopped in front of Ryan's. He was wearing a hoodie and blue jeans, and Mark recognized him from the scene of a number of accidents, triaging. He was maybe twenty-two, if that.

"Hey, Ryan," he said. "So what the hell were you doing

at Gail's tonight? Committing property damage, trying to scare her, hurt her…? What was the plan, to break into her house and drag her out, hang her, kill her? I mean, how far would you have gone if I hadn't shown up?"

Ryan shook his head. "Who says I was even there? I'm not talking to you, Chief. I want my phone call and my lawyer."

"My wife saw you. All those cameras there, and you're telling me you won't accidentally be on one of them?"

There was the hint of a smile. "No, but you will. It's amazing how often you turn on the news and see a cop shooting recklessly into a crowd of concerned citizens. They'll see a danger to the public, unarmed civilians trying to protect their island, nothing else. You should see the news cycle in the morning. I bet your phone will be ringing next, and you'll have no choice but to resign."

Mark had never expected this from Ryan. He'd always thought he was nice. "What happened to you? Who's paying you?"

"Lawyer," was all Ryan said, looking away.

Mark walked down to the next cell, where the two men who had been trying to break in Gail's door were held. One was leaning against the back wall, Hispanic, and the other was lounging on the cot, his dark eyes tracking Mark's steps. "What are your names?"

They both said nothing.

"Okay, listen up, all three of you! The first one who tells me what the hell is going on here and gives me names walks. I want to know who brought you to the island and who is paying you. I need only one of you to talk. Think of the deal this way: You get to keep whatever money you were promised, and you get to walk away. But I'm giving it to only one of you."

There was silence. Mark glanced over to see Carmen

in the doorway. Damn, she looked tired, but not more than he felt. He shoved the key in the lock of the cell and dragged his gaze to the tall, solid dark-haired man on the cot. The other one was shorter, and from his expression, Mark wondered if there was a conscience there. He was hardened, smart.

"You come with me," he said to the one on the cot. His dark hair was cut short, and he had a scar on his right cheek.

"No, I'm fine here," was all he said.

"Come on, not a choice. Get up."

The man stood up and lifted his hands, and Mark stepped back out, waiting for him. The shorter Hispanic man hadn't pulled his hard gaze from his cellmate. Mark locked the cell again and settled his hand on the tall, lanky man's shoulder, leading him past Ryan, who too was watching his every step.

"In my office," Mark said, leading the man, and Carmen followed. Mark patted the chair in front of his desk. "Sit."

The man shook his head. "No, I'm fine."

Mark walked around his desk as Carmen closed the office door and leaned against it. Mark gestured to the chair again. "You don't look fine. In fact, you're in a shitload of trouble. Sit, please." His voice was unusually calm, and he wasn't sure the man would listen. He did. The chair creaked as he sat, and Carmen pulled her arms over her chest, waiting impatiently.

"So, Mister…" Mark started. "You may as well tell me your name. I'm going to find out anyway. Or I could just call you Frank."

The man smiled. "Yeah, I like the name Frank," he said. So he thought it was a game.

"So, Frank, you drew the lucky straw and got your very own get-out-of-jail-free card."

The man frowned and glanced back to Carmen. "Huh?" His brow knit in confusion. "Do you mean you're letting us go?"

Mark didn't bother sitting as he looked down at the man, with no idea where he'd come from. "I'm letting you go. Remember what I said? The first to talk walks. So you get to walk out of here."

"But I didn't talk. I'm not saying anything. I want my lawyer."

Mark shrugged. "What do you need a lawyer for? You're not under arrest. In fact, as soon as we're done here, you get to walk out the door."

Frank had realized what Mark was getting at. "I'm not a snitch. What are you doing?"

Mark glanced to Carmen. "You want to let Ryan and the no-name back there know that I won't be needing to talk to them?"

The chair scooted back sharply, and Frank slapped his hands on Mark's desk. "You can't do that! They'll never believe I talked."

"I think they will. You see, this is how it's going to play out. You're walking out of here. In fact, I'll have Carmen drop you off so you can catch the first ferry off the island at six a.m. Then I'm going to tell your friends you talked. Of course, they won't believe me until they sit there for hours and you don't come back. Now, when I let the guy you were sharing a cell with make his phone call sometime tomorrow, who do you think he'll call?"

The man pulled his hand over his mouth and flicked his dark eyes to Mark. "You'd put a target on me."

"Yeah," Mark said. He nodded and glanced past him again. "Carmen, I think we're done here."

"Wait!" The man shot up. The panic was priceless. "If I tell you everything, they can't know it was from me."

Carmen had her hand on the doorknob. "Sit down, Frank," she said.

"Aston. My name is Aston Bryant."

Okay, now they were getting somewhere.

"Aston, sit down and tell me everything," Mark said, "and I will put you back in that cell, and they will never know it came from you. But I want to know everything, why you were here, who brought you, who paid you. Start talking now."

Aston ran his hand over his face. "We were paid, yeah. Ryan was the contact here, but it was a man named Vasquez who wanted that woman gone. We were being paid higher than a normal rate, a bonus of five hundred."

"Glen Vasquez, by any chance?"

Aston glanced back to Carmen and slowly sat back in his chair, then shrugged. "Sure, sounds about right."

Mark pulled his hand over his chin. A sick feeling burned in his stomach as he thought of a man who controlled too many people on the island. "What were you told to do to Gail?"

Aston hesitated and glanced down. "Whatever it took to get her to leave. Nothing was off the table. Our job was to scare her, to use whatever tactics were needed, to instigate a confrontation, to rally some of the locals to join in, to stir hatred and anger. It's easy when you know what you're doing."

Mark nodded. "So basically, you're telling me you're nothing more than a professional shit-disturber."

Aston said nothing, then shrugged. "Sure."

"Then I think you should explain to me how it works, how it's organized, and how, exactly, you ended up on my island."

"You heard from Mark yet?" Gail said as she pulled out a stool at the island, holding a mug of coffee.

Billy Jo shrugged out of her coat and tossed it over a chair at the table, then tucked her keys in her purse. Her cell phone was in there, and she had wanted to reach for it to call Mark half a dozen times, all because she was freaking out. She turned around, seeing the shadows around Gail's eyes. She was wearing blue jeans and a freshly washed shirt. "No, not yet," she said. "He's handling a lot. I'm sure he'll call soon."

Gail gestured to a pot on the stove. "I made soup for lunch. Figured I could do something. So how did your visit with the doctor go?"

There it was, exactly what Billy Jo didn't want to talk about. She wondered if her face paled as she made herself walk over to the stove and lift the lid of the pot. When she heard Mark's Jeep, she turned to see that Gail had evidently picked up on something. "It was, uh…you know," she said.

"No, I don't know," Gail said. "Good or bad news?"

Mark was talking to someone, and then he whistled. Lucky was already whining and running to the door.

"Not sure," Billy Jo said. "I'll get back to you." She heard the door, the bark of a dog, and looked around the corner to see Lucky sniffing at a familiar lab.

"Hey, babe," Mark said. "Should have called you about the dog. It's Walter's. He was at the house." He closed the door and flicked off the leash. "Couldn't leave him."

The dogs finished sniffing each other, and then the lab walked over to her. She went down to it, letting it lick her face. "So we're keeping him?"

Damn, did Mark ever look tired. She stood up and walked over to him, and he pressed a kiss to her lips, then looked over to Gail behind her. "If it's okay with you," he said. "Otherwise, I'll have to find him a home."

She watched the dog go over to Lucky's water dish and lap up some. Her cat lifted his head from his perch, and the expression on his face was priceless, likely something along the lines of "Seriously, another dog?"

"Why not?" she said. "Another dog is good. So how did it go?"

Mark must have smelled the coffee, as he walked over to it and reached for a mug, then poured some before turning to look at Gail. "We'll pick up some of your things later, but you stay here for a while."

Billy Jo could tell from his expression that something was off. "You may as well spit it out, Mark. How bad is it?"

Mark glanced down to his coffee and then winced as he looked up. "Vasquez hired the protestors, a group of fifteen, through Ryan Cole, who apparently not only volunteers as a medic but is on a payroll for demonstrators. I had no idea how it worked, but according to him, it's organized and promoted online. The tactics are the same. Each protestor has a role. Some are medics, as in Ryan's case, and some are there to go head to head and face the cops. Others are there to create confrontations. The camera is always there to catch everything.

"Then there are ones directing the action on the ground. Apparently, they're well trained, well funded. They're angry, militant, and criminal acts are encouraged to push fear. Gail, you were just a job for them. They incited a few of the residents because they know how to do that with people who are easily swayed. In the meantime, you stay here with us. The people here will cool down. And Vasquez is done. The community is divided. Some will be furious over what he did, but others may support him."

Billy Jo didn't know what to say.

Gail had gripped her mug and then slid it away, saying, "You know what? I'm going to give you two some time to talk. I think I'll go turn the TV on downstairs and watch something. Thanks, Mark." Then she slid off the stool. The lab started following her. She slid her hand over Billy Jo's shoulder and said, "Your turn," before walking away, calling out, "Come on, Sarge! You too, Lucky."

Mark let out a heavy sigh. It really seemed as if he carried the weight of the world.

"It's still nice out," she said. "You want to go sit outside?"

He shook his head. "Would rather grab a shower, a bite to eat, and a few hours of sleep."

Billy Jo took in how tired he looked as he dumped his coffee and started walking to the bedroom. He opened the closet and the gun safe, doing that gun safety check he always did, but he must have known she was in the doorway, as he glanced back to her.

"What's up?" he said as he turned his back again,

tucking his gun and ammo in the safe and locking it. She considered, for a second, saying nothing.

"I went to the doctor this morning."

He shrugged out of his jean jacket and tossed it in the easy chair in the corner, then reached for the badge tucked in the waistband of his jeans and set it on the dresser. Billy Jo leaned against the doorframe and pulled her arms over her chest. She realized he must have figured there was a problem, as he didn't pull his gaze from her now.

"And? Come on, what did he say?" he asked. She made herself pull in a breath as Mark started walking her way. "What's wrong, Billy Jo? Just tell me." He was right in front of her, and she could have reached out and touched him.

"I'm pregnant."

Mark stepped back and ran his hand over his face. He seemed as thrown as she was. "Holy shit! That's fucking fantastic. Damn, I thought something was really wrong with you," he said. Then he lifted her up and swung her around. This was not what she had expected.

"Mark, put me down! What are you doing? This isn't good news."

He put her down. Tired Mark didn't hide his feelings very well. "What are you talking about? Of course this is good news."

She was shaking her head. "How can we consider bringing a child into this world, this fucked-up world where kids disappear? And I'm not exactly a role model for well adjusted."

He said nothing, just pulled his hand over the back of his neck and let out a heavy sigh. Then he reached for her hand, led her to the easy chair in the corner, and said, "Sit down."

She hesitated only a second.

Mark sat on the stool in front of it and reached for her

hands. "Billy Jo, you'll be a great mother. We can't not bring a baby into the world because bad things happen. Yeah, they do, but this is our baby. You aren't responsible for those missing kids. In fact, you being there puts a spotlight on it. You question it and see that it's not brushed under the carpet."

"How can I keep working for them? What Walter said about DCFS… I thought I could make a difference. But everything he said is true."

Mark reached for her hands again, then glanced to the open door and back to her. "Walter left something for me, a thumb drive. I don't know how many other copies there are, a few, but on it is everything, and I mean everything: details about the executives of the foundation he worked for, the companies on the S&P where money has been funneled, payouts to federal and state officials, judges, and politicians, and information on how the money is laundered through non-profits. They say they help the underprivileged, from kids' camps to disaster relief, all kinds of aid. Sure, some of them do provide that help, but only as a front.

"Also on the drive was a document someone put a lot of detail into. It outlines how sixty percent of kids in the foster system are exploited and targeted for trafficking. Because of poor screening and oversight, traffickers are even in the system, with state dollars flowing to them. If you look at states with missing kids, you see communities with sheriffs and politicians who make sure resources are not provided. And that only touches on it. Drugs, big pharma, illegal activity… It's all about money, and it's nothing I can go after." He had just stopped talking, and she felt the weight of what he was carrying.

"What are you going to do?" she said. "I can't in good conscience keep working for the DCFS."

Mark pulled her up and over to him, and she sat on his knee, feeling his arm around her as she slid hers over his shoulder. He looked up to her with those amazing vivid blue eyes. "How can you not keep working for them? If you walk away, how many more kids are going to go missing?" He slid his hand over her stomach. "And this baby is going to be okay. These are the small wins, Billy Jo. With all the awful shit out there, this baby is a gift."

She heard a tap on the doorframe. "Sorry to interrupt," Gail said from the doorway. "Mark, you need to see this."

Billy Jo stood, and so did Mark. They followed Gail out to the living room, where she flicked on the TV and turned up the volume. The scene on the news was of a port outside Long Beach.

"What is this?" Billy Jo said. Mark hadn't pulled his gaze from the screen.

"Over twelve hundred kids were found in a container ship destined for Taiwan," Gail said. "Military or special forces, I think, raided the ship. They found guns, as well."

Mark said nothing, and Billy Jo just stared. The byline said the kids found were all under twelve, and the ship's captain and crew were refusing to cooperate. Mark picked up the remote and flicked off the TV.

"Holy shit, Mark," Billy Jo said.

He turned to her, looking between her and Gail. "That's more than a thousand kids they found."

"Did you know?" Billy Jo asked.

He shook his head. "No. I have a feeling our friend made sure evidence went to the right people."

"Where do you think Walter, Shana, and their daughter are?"

He shook his head and shrugged. "Someplace no one knows about," he said. Then he pulled her close, his arm around her shoulder, and pressed a kiss to the top of her head. "I told you, kids and animals."

She flicked her gaze up to him, feeling his warmth, his strength. Damn, did she love him. "Gail, good news," she said. "We're going to have a baby."

The Sacrifice

COMING NEXT IN THE BILLY JO MCCABE
MYSTERY

Chief Mark Friessen is about to be a family man, with a baby on the way. However, he faces a choice: Either he breaks his word to his wife by taking on a job that will put him in danger, or he stays silent, which would haunt him forever.

Mark lives and dies by his word, and he would do anything for his wife but park his morals and turn his back on those he has sworn to protect, kids and animals, a promise he made to his wife and to himself.

After evidence uncovers a global child trafficking network with ties to his island, Mark is contacted by a secret agency of retired servicemen and cops who ask him to help track down and rescue the children no one is looking for.

The only problem is that Billy Jo is pregnant, and accepting the mission will mean Mark needs to leave her for weeks or months on end. As he struggles with his decision to leave the job he loves and the island that has become his home, he realizes he's at a crossroads. He will need to give everything to save the children, bringing an end to the trafficking of minors, and the elite who prey on them, forever. It's the only way to bring everyone involved to justice.

Yet the kids he's trying to save are not the only ones in danger. When a phone call from home brings everything full circle, Mark's ultimate sacrifice could be Billy Jo and his unborn baby.

Turn the page for a sneak peek of
THE HUNTED the newest release in *THE O'CONNELLS*
Available in print, eBook & audio

The Hunted

THE O'CONNELLS

When two prisoners escape and one is found dead, Marcus O'Connell finds himself being hunted— and the hunter could be someone he trusts.

One late night, Sheriff Marcus O'Connell receives a call about two escaped prisoners considered a danger to the community. A search is underway, and the warden has reason to believe the escaped convicts are headed toward Livingston. An urgent warning is issued: Shoot to kill.

Hours later, Marcus is called to a crime scene. The body of one of the escaped prisoners has been discovered deep in the woods, and the scene has already been lit up, with three prison guards standing over the body, along with the sheriff and deputy from the county over and a tracker with his dogs. A story has been neatly put together, and the group at the scene tries to send Marcus on his way.

Yet one prisoner is still missing. Marcus is told no investigation is necessary, that he should sign off on the case and walk away. But nothing adds up. The problem is that dead men can't talk, and Marcus can't shake the feeling that the story he's being told is a coverup for something far more sinister.

The Hunted

CHAPTER 1

The sound of crickets punctuated the quiet neighborhood. Darkness had settled in, but Marcus needed a minute, as he leaned against the large porch beam, before he could lock up for the night and feel that all was okay in his part of the world. He lifted his hand in a wave to his brother Owen and his wife, Tessa, as they drove away in her small compact. Again, he took in the neighbors' houses. Next door, the lights were off and all seemed quiet.

Ryan and Jenny were already inside their house across the road, and the outside light was now off. Marcus waited for that feeling he got every night before locking up, an assurance that it would be okay for him to lay his head down and go to sleep. He counted heads, making sure everyone was okay, listening to the sounds inside his house, the fussing of Cameron, who was doing his nightly protest against going to sleep.

The screen door squeaked open behind him, and Marcus turned to see his dad step out, wearing blue jeans and a black t-shirt. He heard his mom and Reine talking inside. His dad nodded to him and headed over.

"Your mom is finishing up in the kitchen with Reine and Eva," Raymond said. "That boy of yours is just like you. You always fought your mom and argued every night about how you weren't tired, but a second later you'd be out cold. You didn't know how to stop."

Marcus turned to look back at the street. He was still trying to understand his dad. He leaned against the post on the porch, breathing in the warm summer night. The smell told him tomorrow would be another hot day.

"You were rather quiet tonight," Raymond said. "Everything okay?"

What was he supposed to say? This feeling had come out of nowhere. He couldn't remember ever having felt so unsettled, and he didn't have a clue what had caused it—family, life, something else?

"Just one of those days, you know," Marcus said, unable to find words to explain it.

His dad only nodded. It wasn't lost on Marcus that his dad had been forced to stick around Livingston because his mom had refused to leave her children and grandkids. His dad had a way of seeing everything. Marcus had figured that much out, but a stranger wouldn't have been able to tell, as Raymond never let his gaze linger too long.

Now he did, narrowing his eyes, peering out into the darkness. The stars were out, and a few streetlights were on. "Always the sheriff, looking out to make sure everyone is tucked in, safe," he said. "Expecting trouble?"

Marcus looked over to his dad. Inside, the house phone was ringing, and a second later, it was answered. "You know something I don't?" he said. The sarcasm dripped.

His dad only shrugged. Marcus heard footsteps and pushed away from the post just as the screen door squeaked again, and Reine stepped out, her dark hair pulled back, wearing a peach sundress, barefoot.

"Marcus, it's for you," she said. "It's Therese." She held out the cordless phone.

Marcus didn't look over to his dad, who he knew was watching him in the way only Raymond O'Connell could. Marcus took the portable phone. "Thanks, Reine," he said, then waited as she walked back in the house. He put the phone to his ear, glancing only once to his dad, knowing his deputy called only if there was something he needed to handle. "What's up, Therese?"

"Sorry to call so late, Sheriff, but I have a message from the warden from Montana State. Two prisoners have escaped, and all he said was that they could be headed this way. I was about to call him back…" There was static on the line. His deputy was cutting in and out, as if she were driving.

"Hey, Therese, you're cutting out. You said two prisoners escaped from Montana State?" He was already walking back into the house and taking the stairs two at a time. Upstairs, Charlotte was reading to his son, whom he thought he heard jumping on his bed. Marcus was in his bedroom now, yanking open the closet door and opening the gun safe to retrieve his .357 SIG.

"Sorry, Sheriff," Therese said. "I'm about twenty minutes away, and the cell service is like shit out here. Picked up the message on the way. All it said was that two prisoners escaped. The warden is…"

"Kellogg," Marcus cut in, fastening the holstered gun to the waistband of his jeans. As he closed up the gun safe, he pictured a man he'd met only a few times.

"I missed that part of the message," Therese said. "I'll give him a call and let you know what he says."

Marcus glanced to the open door. His wife now stood

in the doorway. "No, Therese, I've got it," he said. "I'll have Charlotte check the message, and I'll give the warden a call."

She said nothing, and he noted her hesitation.

"Anything else?" he said, realizing it had come out rather short.

"No, that was all," Therese said. "You sure, Sheriff? I don't mind making the call. It may be nothing."

"Or it may be a lot," he said. "No, I've got this one." Then he hung up and held the phone out to Charlotte, taking in her wide eyes.

"What's going on, Marcus?"

He reached for his badge. "Prison break or something along those lines. Therese just called, said the warden at Montana State left a message. Two prisoners. I need you to get his number and play that message for me."

She was already nodding and dialing the office. Something about his wife handling phones and dispatching again settled him in ways he couldn't explain. She scribbled down the number on a pad of paper on the dresser just as his two-year-old son came running in, all smiles, appearing nowhere near ready to go to sleep.

Marcus reached for him and gave him a toss in the air, then held him and kissed his cheek. "Hey, you. Giving your mom a hard time? You're supposed to be asleep."

"Not tired."

"Yeah, well, you will be soon. Go get a book and get in bed."

"Here, Marcus, the number," Charlotte said. "The message is kind of garbled, but yes, it's something about two prisoners escaping."

He put Cameron down after kissing him again and reached for the paper and the phone, shaking his head over his rambunctious son.

Charlotte shook her head. "He's going to be the end of me. You know he argues every night about how he isn't tired?" She pulled her arms over her faded green t-shirt, her dark hair pulled up in a ponytail. "You're heading out, aren't you?"

"Yeah, after I call the warden," he said. "I don't like this."

There it was, that smile of hers he loved. She leaned in the doorway, glancing once over her shoulder down the hall to where their son's bedroom was as he dialed the phone.

"Montana State, warden's office." The voice was muffled, and Marcus had to really listen past the rough twang.

"This is Sheriff O'Connell, from Livingston. Is the warden there? I've got a message from him about a prison escape."

He heard a rustle on the other end, then a clunk. Evidently, whoever had answered barely knew how to use a phone. "Yeah, yeah," the person said, then yelled out, "Warden! Call for you from that Sheriff O'Connell."

Marcus reached for his wallet and stuffed it in his back pocket, then reached for his duty belt. Charlotte didn't look away, gesturing for an explanation, but Marcus only shook his head. There was another rustle on the phone.

"Sheriff? Warden Kellogg here." The man had a deep voice. "Afraid two prisoners escaped. Was discovered only a short time ago by one of the guards. We're in lockdown now. Just finished a count and are interrogating some prisoners. We know two got out for sure, but how, we have no idea. They likely had help from inside. I suspect they could be headed your way. These men are dangerous, both of them. I've already contacted state officials, as well, along with the other sheriffs in the area. An order has already been issued: Shoot to kill."

Marcus angled his head, looking right at Charlotte. He wasn't sure he'd heard the warden correctly. "You can't be serious," he said. "Who authorized that order? With all due respect, Warden, capturing the prisoners is the first priority."

"Sheriff O'Connell, these prisoners are a danger to the community," the warden said. "They will slit your throat and kill you without a second thought. If you want to dance around them and be the nice guy, do it on your own time and not at the detriment of the good people of Montana. You see them, you shoot them, because these two will do anything and everything to avoid capture. Killing, maiming, looting, burning. You want the details of what they'd do to your wife and sisters, everyone in your family, everyone you care about? If you want to argue with me about bringing them in alive, you can do it, but I don't want these two getting anywhere near innocent people. I've already reached out to Judge Harris, and photos of the prisoners have been sent to you."

Marcus didn't have a clue who these two prisoners were or what they'd done, but that sick feeling was back in his stomach with the image of the horror the warden had painted. Damn, what kind of evil had the two men done?

On the other end, the warden was talking to someone else. Then he addressed Marcus again. "Anything else, Sheriff? If not, I suggest you get your ass out there and start looking. Stan has faxed over the photos, and emails have gone out statewide."

Something about Warden Kellogg had always unsettled Marcus, but he couldn't put his finger on what it was. "Yeah, you said they could be headed my way. Why is that?

They have family, friends, contacts here? I need all that information."

"Everything about both prisoners has been sent to you. One has a girlfriend, I understand, outside Livingston, and a brother up toward Billings. If that's all, Sheriff, I've got a fucking mess to handle here. You have any questions, get in touch with Sheriff Lester up in Stillwater County. He's got more on them, and he's been on this since word went out. And, Sheriff O'Connell? A word of advice. I understand you may want to give these men a second chance, but sometimes we're all better off if a criminal is six feet under. You understand?"

Yeah, he understood, but a knot twisted in his stomach as he looked over to his wife. He wondered if this explained the sick feeling he had or the cold sweat that had broken out up his spine. "Understood," he said. "I'll start looking." Then he hung up and tossed the phone on the bed.

"What is it, Marcus?"

Marcus counted the extra clips in his duty belt, then walked over to his wife and ran his hand over her shoulder. "Warden says the prisoners had help from the inside to get out. Says they're dangerous. Photos have been faxed and emailed. Can you access those? I'm going to ask Mom and Dad to stay until I get back," he said. It was just a feeling he had, the need to keep his family together. "See if you can pull up the prisoners' files, too. Warden said they've been sent. I want to know everything about them: who they are, what they did, and exactly how dangerous they are."

He hurried down the stairs, and Charlotte was right behind him. Raymond was back in the house, and he could hear his mom, Reine, and Eva in the kitchen.

Marcus stepped off the bottom step, and Charlotte moved around him into the living room, over to the small desk where her laptop was.

"What's going on?" Raymond said as Marcus reached for his sheriff's jacket and lifted it from the hook.

"Marcus, I just sent the photos and files to your phone," Charlotte called out.

Marcus pulled his iPhone from his coat pocket and turned to his dad. "Can you and Mom stay?"

Raymond didn't seem surprised. He only nodded and said, "Yeah, of course. You worried about something?"

Marcus pulled out the keys to his cruiser. "Two prisoners have escaped and could be headed this way. Warden says they're dangerous, so much so that he wants us to shoot first and ask questions later, so I don't want to leave Charlotte, Reine, and the kids alone."

He knew his dad understood. "Yeah, you got it," he said. "You be careful."

Marcus thumbed through his phone and pulled up the photos his wife had sent. One was dark skinned, the other lighter, both with dark hair and brown eyes, the same bugged-out mugshot expressions. Their names were Rafe Jackson and Holter Donnelly. "Charlotte, send these to Harold and Ryan, too," he called out over his shoulder as he opened the door, and his dad was right behind him, holding the inside screen. "Charlotte has the photos," Marcus told him. "Take a good look."

Raymond nodded. "I'll call Ryan and Owen," he said.

Marcus lingered just outside. He didn't know what to say to his dad. Out of anyone, he knew Raymond had a handle on this. "Thanks," he finally said, then started down the steps. He heard the door close behind him and the lock flick closed.

He dialed his cell phone, walking straight for his cruiser and climbing in. As he tossed his duty belt and coat on the passenger seat, the phone rang once, twice…

"Okay, what did you forget?" Suzanne answered. He thought he heard Arnie fussing in the background.

"Put Harold on," he said, shoving his cell phone in the mount on the dash. He started the car.

"No can do," Suzanne said. "He's in the shower. What is it?"

There she went, playing interference. He knew she was still pissed at him because he wouldn't let her play cop in his county.

"You tell Harold to get the hell out of the shower and call me back," he said. "There was a prison break. This is serious shit, Suzanne. Charlotte just sent him the photos and files. I need him to dig into it and then meet me at the office. I'm not messing around. Have him call me. Can you do that?"

She was quiet for a second. "Don't take my head off, Marcus. Yeah, I'll tell him. Hey, big brother?" She always seemed to need to have the last word.

"What?" he said as he backed the cruiser out, ready to get off the phone. He flicked on the headlights and gave the vehicle gas, looking out into the darkness, knowing he'd be taking a second and third look at anyone he saw that night, scrutinizing who they were and what they were doing.

"Watch your back," she said.

He felt a smile tug at the corners of his lips. "Always do," he said. "Now have Harold call me."

Marcus ended the call before his sister could add one more thing. As he rounded the corner, feeling his own angst, he drove slower than usual and took a good, long look at the few pickups parked along the street, scanning for anyone out walking. There was only a couple with a dog.

This was going to be a really long night.

"Lorhainne Eckhart is one of my go to authors when I want a guaranteed good book. So many twists and turns, but also so much love and such a strong sense of family."

(LORA W., REVIEWER)

New York Times & USA Today bestseller Lorhainne Eckhart is best known for writing Raw Relatable Real Romance where "Morals and family are running themes." As one fan calls her, she is the "Queen of the family saga." (aherman) writing "the ups and downs of what goes on within a family but also with some suspense, angst and of course a bit of romance thrown in for good measure."

Follow Lorhainne on Bookbub to receive alerts on New Releases and Sales and join her mailing list at Lorhainne-Eckhart.com for her Monday Blog, all book news, give-aways and FREE reads. With over 120 books, audiobooks, and multiple series published and available at all, retailers now translated into six languages. She is a multiple recipient of the Readers' Favorite Award for Suspense and Romance, and lives in the Pacific Northwest on an island, is the mother of three, her oldest has autism and she is an advocate for never giving up on your dreams.

"Lorhainne Eckhart has this uncanny way of just hitting the spot every time with her books."

(CAROLINE L., REVIEWER)

The O'Connells: *The O'Connells of Livingston, Montana are not your typical family. A riveting collection of stories surrounding the ups and downs of what goes on within a family but also with some suspense, angst and of course a bit of romance thrown in for good measure. "I thought I loved the Friessens, but I absolutely adore the O'Con-nell's. Each and every book has different genres of stories, but the one thing in common is how she is able to wrap it around the family, which is the heart of each story." (C. Logue)*

The Friessens: *An emotional big family romance series, the Friessen family siblings find their relationships tested, lay their hearts on the line, and discover lasting love! "Lorhainne Eckhart is one of my go to authors when I want* *a guaranteed good book. So many twists and turns, but also so much love and such a strong sense of family." (Lora W., Reviewer)*

The Parker Sisters: *The Parker Sisters are a close-knit family, and like any other family they have their ups and downs. Eckhart has crafted another intense family drama… "The character development is outstanding, and the emotional investment is high…" (Aherman, Reviewer)*

The McCabe Brothers: *Join the five McCabe siblings on their journeys to the dark and dangerous side of love! An intense, exhilarating collection of romantic thrillers you won't want to miss. — "Eckhart has a new series that is definitely worth the read. The queen of the family saga started this series with a spin-off of her wildly successful Friessen series." From a Readers' Favorite award—winning author and "queen of the family saga" (Aherman)*

Lorhainne loves to hear from her readers! You can connect with me at:
www.LorhainneEckhart.com
lorhainneeckhart.le@gmail.com

In the Family
In the Silence
In the Charm
Unexpected Consequences
It Was Always You
The First Time I Saw You
Welcome to My Arms
Welcome to Boston
I'll Always Love You
Ground Rules
A Reason to Breathe
You Are My Everything
Anything For You
The Homecoming
Stay Away From My Daughter
The Bad Boy
A Place of Our Own
The Visitor
All About Devon
Long Past Dawn
How to Heal a Heart
Keep Me In Your Heart

The O'Connells

The Neighbor
The Third Call
The Secret Husband
The Quiet Day
The Commitment
The Missing Father
The Hometown Hero
Justice
The Family Secret

The Fallen O'Connell
The Return of the O'Connells
And The She Was Gone
The Stalker
The O'Connell Family Christmas
The Girl Next Door
Broken Promises
The Gatekeeper
The Hunted

The McCabe Brothers

Don't Stop Me (Vic)
Don't Catch Me (Chase)
Don't Run From Me (Aaron)
Don't Hide From Me (Luc)
Don't Leave Me (Claudia)
Out of Time

A Billy Jo McCabe Mystery

Nothing As it Seems
Hiding in Plain Sight
The Cold Case
The Trap
Above the Law
The Stranger at the Door
The Children
The Last Stand
The Charity

The Wilde Brothers

The One (Joe and Margaret)
The Honeymoon, A Wilde Brothers Short
Friendly Fire (Logan and Julia)

Not Quite Married, A Wilde Brothers Short
A Matter of Trust (Ben and Carrie)
The Reckoning, A Wilde Brothers Christmas
Traded (Jake)
Unforgiven (Samuel)
The Holiday Bride

Married in Montana

His Promise
Love's Promise
A Promise of Forever

The Parker Sisters

Thrill of the Chase
The Dating Game
Play Hard to Get
What We Can't Have
Go Your Own Way
A June Wedding

Kate & Walker

One Night
Edge of Night
Last Night

Walk the Right Road Series

The Choice
Lost and Found
Merkaba
Bounty
Blown Away: The Final Chapter
He Came Back

The Saved Series

Saved
Vanished
Captured

Single Titles
Loving Christine

www.ingramcontent.com/pod-product-compliance
Lightning Source LLC
Chambersburg PA
CBHW030956210726
48290CB00007B/2340